Death of A Commuter

By the Same Author:

DEATH OF A COMMUTER

by Leo Bruce

Published in 1988 by
Academy Chicago Publishers
213 West Institute Place
Chicago, Illinois 60610

Copyright © Leo Bruce, 1967

Printed and bound in the USA

No part of this book may be reproduced in
any form without the express written
permission of the publisher.

Library of Congress Cataloging-in-Publication Data

Bruce, Leo, 1903-1980
    Death of a commuter.

    I. Title.
PR6005.R673D43   1988   823'.912   88-24194
ISBN 0-89733-326-8 (pbk.)

To
Cameron Rougvie
whose thrillers thrill and
whose mysteries mystify

Chapter One

FIVE MEN OCCUPIED THEIR USUAL PLACES IN A FIRST-CLASS carriage, but the sixth place was empty.

This seemed to cause some disquiet to those present. One watched the platform, another glanced at his wristwatch. It was clearly an unusual occurrence.

Dogman broke the silence. He was sitting next to the empty place. His check suit and striped tie lacked the restraint evident in the dark suits of the others and no one welcomed his inquiry for it was unusual to exchange remarks until one pipe had been smoked and the newspaper read—about half-way to London. But Dogman, conventional though he might appear to others, had never quite conformed to the etiquette of group commuting.

" I wonder what's happened to Parador," he said brightly.

Thriver, a wizened solicitor frowned and picked up his paper. He had never approved of Dogman, a bookmaker, and did not know how he had managed to thrust himself into this company. But James Rumble was more polite.

" Overslept, perhaps," he said gruffly. He was a partner in a large travel agency and considered rather a man of the world.

The brothers Limpole who occupied the other two seats said nothing at all. They never wasted words, or anything else.

The missing man, a certain Felix Parador, was a jaunty near-millionaire in his sixties, generous and popular but full of personal prejudices. It seemed to all of them extraordinary that he should be missing.

Every weekday morning since the end of the summer holiday season the six of them had shared this compartment on the 8.52, the fast city train from the new town of Brenstead. Every morning they had exchanged the same gruff scarcely audible greetings and indulged in a few words of general conversation towards the end of the journey. They knew one another's little ways, how Thriver kept a small velvet pad in his overcoat pocket with which to re-polish his brilliant shoes as they came into London, how the elder Limpole, Charles, would read the paper through then hand it over to Edward to avoid the expense of two newspapers, how James Rumble smoked a pipe and Willy James Dogman a cheroot.

Perhaps if two of them met in Brenstead or in the presence of their wives there might be some chit-chat exchanged, or something as closely personal as an enquiry after health. But not in the morning. Not in that compartment. The nearest they had ever gone towards intimacy was an exchange of comments on last night's television. Felix Parador did *The Times* crossword and made history one morning by asking Thriver to lend him a pencil or pen, accepting it with a silent nod. Yet when one of them was absent they were none of them at ease. Perhaps, though it was probably no more than a missed train, it reminded them of human mortality and the evanescence of their own lives, insisting to each uncomfortably that one morning his seat too, would be empty.

Then an unprecedented thing happened. The sliding door was pushed back and a man entered. He was a strange-looking man, too, dressed in black, with black tie and socks. If he had worn a silk hat he might have been an undertaker. Except for his heavy dark glasses. Undertakers do not wear dark glasses.

At first everyone was too dumbfounded to speak. Intruders

were unheard of here. But when the man prepared to sit down Willy James Dogman found his voice.

" That seat's taken," he said.

The man had a curiously deep voice which made his words sound impressive.

" *He won't be coming,*" he said.

No one pretended any longer to be immersed in his newspaper. But they left it to Dogman to go farther.

" What do you mean?" Dogman asked the intruder.

" Just that. *He won't be coming.*"

Damnable to have to listen to someone wearing dark glasses. You can never tell whom, exactly, he's addressing.

" How do *you* know?" asked Dogman.

The intruder hesitated a moment. The question seemed to have baffled him. Then he looked up to see that the train was beginning to move. He nodded towards the platform.

" Well, will he?" he asked.

This left everyone with the uncomfortable feeling that he had meant something else. Somehow one felt that this mysterious man knew who was missing, knew why he was not there, knew where he was.

Dogman bashed on regardless.

" Do you know Mr. Parador?" he asked.

" I didn't know the gentleman's name," said the intruder.

" But you do now?"

" You've just told me."

Dogman looked about him at the now preoccupied expressions on the faces of his travelling companions. What more was there to say? he seemed to ask. The intruder drew a folded newspaper from his pocket and began to read. It was the most uncomfortable journey any of them had ever passed.

Fifteen minutes from London, Dogman made an effort to rouse his fellow-travellers to their usual exchange of casual remarks.

" Hear about Hopelady and the bell?" Rev. George Hopelady was the Vicar of Brenstead and famous as a practical joker. " He muffled old Gobler's bell before practice the other night

9

and the poor old chap was nearly breaking his heart trying to make it chime." Dogman made expressive gestures. "Pulling away," he explained.

"Disgraceful. A minister," said Charles Limpole.

"Oh well. You know Hopelady."

"I certainly do not. He is not at all the sort of man I should wish to know. A mocking sort of fellow who holds nothing sacred."

"We don't attend the parish church," Edward Limpole put in.

There were a few uneasy glances towards the intruder but he took no part in what little conversation there was and when the train came into the great London terminus of Padoria Cross he prepared to leave like the rest of them in silence. Before they had all left the carriage he had melted into the crowd intent on reaching their places of business.

"'Straordinary, that fellow getting into our carriage," said Thriver to Rumble as they walked towards the platform exit together.

"'Straordinary," agreed Rumble and left it at that. With a nod they parted.

Meanwhile Police Officer Brophy, as he insisted on being addressed, was wheeling his bicycle up Downaway Hill towards the Great Ring. This was a beauty spot ten miles from Brenstead which was famous not only in the district but throughout the south of England. Less beautiful than Chanctonbury Ring and less impressive than Stonehenge it still drew many visitors during the summer months to look out over the astonishing coloured map which England seemed to become from its height. The landscape was in some way etherealised from the Great Ring, its blotches wiped out, its pylons inoffensive, its roadside hoardings invisible, its corrugated iron roofs blending with tiled roofs and its bungalows concealed. One could believe England was still an agricultural country.

From the main road up Downaway Hill a narrower road ran to the parking place below the Great Ring. This was enormous but some cunning County Council official had had the wit to approve plans which made it invisible from the Great Ring itself. Moreover though the concession for a café had been applied for and there had been bitter correspondence in the local paper, no building was allowed and only a movable stall appeared on summer afternoons.

Police Officer Brophy reached the side-turning which led up to the Great Ring and hesitated. It was part of his patrol duties to inspect the car park and the Great Ring itself but he was anxious to reach the top of Downaway Hill where comfort awaited him at the back door of the The Three Thistles. But his conscience won and he made the ascent.

It was as well he did, he reflected later. For in the car park was a car, and in the car was a dead man.

Police Officer Brophy saw the car from a hundred yards away. He saw that it was red and frosted over, looking like a huge frosted cherry. It seemed to have been there for at least the most part of the night. Only when he opened the door beside the driving seat did he get the full shock of surprise because then the body of a middle-aged man, stiff as a poker as he said afterwards, almost fell in his arms.

Police Officer Brophy kept his head. Using considerable strength he pushed the stiff corpse back in its place and slammed the door. His duty was clear. First to inform, then to stand guard over the car until an investigating team should arrive. But to inform he would have to continue on his way to The Three Thistles since there was no other building in the neighbourhood.

It was nearing 10 a.m. when he reached the pub and knocked importantly on the door.

"Can I use your telephone, Mr. Diggs?" he asked, discouraging by the urgency in his manner any immediate offer of hospitality.

Police Officer Brophy knew that unfortunately Sergeant Beckett would be on duty, a man he particularly disliked for what he considered his petty and condescending superiority.

"Police Officer Brophy, here," he said when he had got through.

" Yes, Brophy, what is it?" said Beckett hurriedly.

" I'm speaking from The Three Thistles public house . . ."

" Hotel," put in Mr. Diggs.

" What are you doing there?" asked the sergeant.

" I have just discovered in the car park of the Great Ring a frozen-over car with a dead man in it."

" How do you know he's dead?"

Brophy tried to keep his temper. " He was cold," he said sulkily.

" So would you be if you'd been out at the Great Ring all night. What's he look like?"

" I didn't wait to take notes on his appearance . . ."

" You should have. Young or old?"

" Middle-aged, I should say. I came to report the matter at once."

" Better get back there and wait till the van comes. Shouldn't be left even for a moment. You may find it gone when you get back, so don't waste time now."

Mr. Diggs shook his head in sympathy.

" That's what they're like," he said. " Going to have a quick one?"

" It must be quick then," said Brophy who knew that Mr. Diggs had allowed some customers to stay in the back room till nearly midnight.

" Short, you mean?"

" Have to be."

" Scotch?"

" Gin. With a drop of pep in it. Anyone in last night, unusual, I mean?"

" Not to say unusual. No, there wasn't. You mean about this you were phoning about? No, nothing I noticed. We had one or two in. Nothing special."

" I expect you'll be interrogated later."

" Me? What for?"

" Nearest habitation. It's my opinion there's something dodgy about this. Very dodgy, if you ask me. Shouldn't be surprised if we had a big case on our hands." Then, somewhat inconsequently, "He was as stiff as a poker. Must have been there all night."

"We never heard anything," said Mr. Diggs. "You'd think we would have, wouldn't you? It can't be more than a quarter of a mile away. You don't mean you think it was murder or anything like that?"

"I'm not giving any opinion at the moment. I must be getting back."

Police Officer Brophy was able to freewheel back to the side road which led to the Great Ring and was relieved to see that the car was where he left it. Moreover as he saw by peering in, the corpse was still at the driving seat. There was nothing to do now but wait for the van.

It was twenty minutes before he saw the cavalcade approaching—an ambulance and two cars.

"Looks to me like murder, Sir," he ventured to remark to Sergeant Beckett.

The sergeant did not bother to answer this, but giving Brophy what is aptly called a withering look he strode forward to the red car. Brophy prepared to watch the intricate proceedings which he knew would follow, doctor's examination, photographs, fingerprint check, a search of the car and of the dead man's pockets and person before the body would be sent in for more careful examination. But he didn't see all this.

"Go down to the road, Brophy, and don't let anything up here at all," said Beckett heartlessly, and Brophy turned to obey. You had to be a long time in the police, he reflected bitterly, before you were good enough to handle a corpse.

News, when it reached him in the canteen from a police officer younger than himself who had had nothing to do with finding the cadaver, was disappointing. The body was that of a man named Felix Parador who had not been home since he left for London on the previous morning. His wife had not expected him home last night as he had telephoned to say he would stay in town, but the man in charge of the car park at the station had seen him drive away after the train in at 6.45.

It appeared that he had driven out to the Great Ring for some

13

reason and there quietly taken an overdose of antibiotic sleeping pills called Opilactic, since an empty bottle which had contained these was beside him and one of the pills was even found on the floor. He also had in his right hand a silver drinking-flask which had contained whisky and it was thought that he had used this to help him swallow the pills. It was impossible to say at what time he had died last night but medical opinion put it somewhere between eight and eleven. The official police opinion was, Brophy heard from his friend who confided it in a low voice, that the man had committed suicide. No reason for it had as yet been hazarded but there had been some talk in Brenstead about his wife.

Police Officer Brophy felt indignant at having been left out of this.

" Who found the bloody thing? That's what I should like to know!" he exclaimed rhetorically. " That's what you get for being conscientious. Next time I shall let them find it themselves!"

His friend looked serious.

" How do you know there'll be a next time?" he asked, and his words were remembered later.

The evening papers carried a short account of the event, part news paragraph, part obituary. Mr. Felix Parador of The Old Manor, Brenstead . . . company director (that useful term used for any petty criminal or for millionaire initiators of take-over bids) found early this morning . . . the Norsex police say foul play not suspected . . . A few lines of shrugging and impersonal reading matter while even then preparations were being made for a post-mortem.

The Norsex police might not suspect foul play but the people of Brenstead considered themselves less simple-minded. ' It stands to reason,' they said, and ' Who's going to believe?' they asked. There was a certain amount of wishful thinking in this for little is more teasing than to have a promising piece of sensational scandal dashed before it was fairly started. There must have been more to it than that, they said. Why, they had seen Mr. Parador only that morning or the previous day and he had *said nothing then*. And what about Mrs. Parador? Everyone knew about her. And if he wanted to commit suicide why should he go out to the Great Ring? That was the question.

Perhaps the inquest would tell something. It was held two days later in the ballroom of The Royal Oak. The coroner, a dignified but shrewd individual who asked searching questions, heard the medical evidence unmoved. Death had been caused by an over-dose of the drug which was the basic ingredient of Opilactic. The doctors who had carried out the post-mortem had no doubt of that. As to the time of death they admitted uncertainty. The dose must have been a massive one, so many grammes of so and so and a lot of technical terminology about ' the organs '. The widow, who was offered every consideration and the sympathy of the court, had no explanation of her husband's conduct. He had been in excellent spirits when he left her that morning. No, she had not been surprised when he telephoned from his office to say he would not be home for the night. He had done that on previous occasions, though not lately. She *was* surprised to hear he had come down on his usual train after all without letting her know. He was very punctilious in such matters.

His brother, Magnus Parador, had been more truculent. His brother's affairs had been in excellent order and he for one did not believe that Felix would ever have committed suicide, unless he had become suddenly deranged, which was most unlikely. He was the sanest man Magnus Parador had ever known. But had he not been a prisoner of the Japanese for two years? Yes, but there were no ill effects of that noticeable now.

The only evidence which seemed to help the coroner was that of a clerk in Parador's office, Philip Dukes. Yes, he thought Mr. Parador had behaved oddly that afternoon. He had taken the wrong hat and finding it far too small for him had larked about in it before returning it to its hook. What did he mean by larking about? Well, he had put it on his head, grinned to him, Dukes, and seemed to make a joke of it. No one else had noticed this, but it was enough for the coroner. The verdict was Suicide While the Balance of his Mind was Disturbed. Foul play, it was seen, was not suspected and the post-mortemised body of

15

Felix Parador was buried in an honourable grave. The five men who travelled daily with him looked out for a candidate for his seat in the compartment. Slowly and unwillingly the people of Brenstead turned to other matters.

Chapter Two

ON THE LAST DAY OF THE SPRING TERM CAROLUS DEENE, THE senior history master of the Queen's School, Newminster, returned gratefully to his small house in the town. Not for four weeks would he hear the booming voice of his headmaster whose speech was full of platitudes and pomposity, nor have his class disturbed by awkward questions from a difficult boy named Simmons. In spite of what he considered a vulgarly large private income he took his work as a schoolmaster seriously. He had been grateful for the chance of filling his time and his mind when he had first been released in 1946 from his war service with the Commandos, for his young wife had died during the war. He was grateful to it still. But he was not above having what is common to boys and masters—an end-of-term feeling.

His hobby—he insisted that it was no more—was the investigation of crime and he had been astonishingly successful in disentangling the evidence in a number of sensational cases. He worked anonymously, both because he preferred to do so and because the headmaster of his school insisted that he should, lest, as he put it, 'the fair name of The Queen's School should become sullied '. But from the point of view of investigation it had been an uneventful term. Nothing had happened to rouse his curiosity for several months.

Two people, he knew, were delighted at this, the headmaster, Hugh Gorringer, and his housekeeper, Mrs. Stick. The headmaster had gone so far as to say so when they had parted today. A large man with immense red hairy ears and a far too evident belief in his own importance, he had unbent to address Carolus privately.

" I cannot but admit, my dear Deene, that I have felt considerable relief of late to note that your unfortunate hobby has not been in evidence. As you know, it is a matter of concern to me when you become involved in some sordid investigation far better left to the proper authorities. It is some months, if I mistake me not, since we have heard the tocsin."

As for Mrs. Stick, she expressed her pleasure quite openly.

" I was only saying to Stick," she had told Carolus a week ago, " it's a long time now since we were mixed up in one of those nasty murder cases. It's been quite a relief. I don't have to wonder what my sister in Battersea's thinking half the time or have my heart jump in my mouth every time the door bell rings."

But when Carolus had sunk into his favourite arm-chair that afternoon and Mrs. Stick had set the tea-tray beside him, he felt far from relieved. The holiday that stretched out in front of him seemed dull in prospect. He wanted something to do. A nice neat little murder, perhaps, with a bevy of promising suspects or even one of those clumsy loutish ones which were often, in his experience, the most puzzling. He ate a couple of crumpets spread with anchovy paste and finished his cup of China tea thoughtfully. There was nothing to interest him in the evening paper.

When Mrs. Stick came to get the tray, however, he saw that the little woman had something on her mind. Her thin lips were tightly set and her steel-rimmed glasses seemed to flash ominously.

" Stick wants a word with you," she said.

" *Stick* does?" It was a fatuous question but the situation was unprecedented. Stick never wanted a word with anyone. If he had any desires or interests at all they were interpreted by Mrs. Stick.

"That's what he says. It's nothing to do with me," Mrs. Stick continued. "I've told him to let sleeping dogs lie, but there you are." She turned to the door. "You better come in and tell Mr. Deene what you want," she called to her waiting husband.

Stick entered.

"Yes, Stick?"

"It's like this," said Stick, and stopped.

"It's about the gentleman he used to work for," said Mrs. Stick.

"That's it," corroborated Stick.

"There's been something about him in the papers," Mrs. Stick explained unwillingly.

"Ah," said Stick.

"I don't know why he wants to bother you with it, sir, but he would have it you must know. Tell Mr. Deene what's happened."

Stick made an effort.

"He's dead," he managed.

"Well, we've all got to die," said Carolus profoundly.

"That's what I told him. Only he's very obstinate about it. This gentleman's done for himself. There's been an inquest and everything."

"That's where it is. I don't believe it," said Stick. "Not Mr. Parador."

"Parador?" said Carolus. "Yes, I read that case. You used to work for him, did you?"

"Yes, and knew him well. He wasn't the man for anything of that sort. What's more his brother doesn't think so either."

"How do you know?"

"I've seen him. He lives over Latchfield way. I've been over to see him."

"You see?" said Mrs. Stick. "Once he gets something into his head there's no stopping him. It's not as though it's any business of his."

"But it is, in a way. There's something for me in his will. Mr. Magnus told me so."

19

" All the more reason to keep out of it. You'll find yourself a suspect next."

" Why are you so certain about this?" asked Carolus gently.

" Stands to reason, doesn't it? Found in his car with an empty bottle of these sleeping tablets. Who put them there, that's what I'd like to know."

" Coroners are no fools," said Carolus, feeling himself grow more and more sententious. " If there had been the slightest reason for suspicion . . ."

" I'm suspicious, anyway," said Stick obstinately. " I knew the gentleman. I'm not saying he couldn't have been driven to it by his wife. That could happen to anyone."

" You better be careful what you're saying," put in Mrs. Stick. Stick continued as though he had not heard.

" But in this case his brother, that's Mr. Magnus Parador, says she was a very nice woman. He knew them both. Didn't nag him or anything."

" Stick!"

" So that wasn't what done it. There's something funny about it."

" What do you want me to do?" asked Carolus.

" He doesn't want you to do anything, sir. With you just starting your holiday. Ten to one if you was to get mixed up in it there'd be half a dozen murders before you could say knife."

" All the same, I should like to know," said Stick tenaciously.

" You say his brother thinks there may be something wrong?"

" He's pretty well sure of it. Why don't you pop over and see him?"

" Perhaps I will."

" There. I told you what would come of it," said Mrs. Stick desperately. " Now see what you've done."

" You can't have someone done for without saying a word, can you, sir?" Stick appealed to Carolus. " When would you be thinking of going?"

" Tomorrow morning, perhaps. If you've got his number I'll ring him this evening. After dinner," added Carolus, seeing Mrs. Stick's face.

"I was going to say." Mrs. Stick looked more severe than ever. "Just when I've got some nice Cocky Saint Jacks for you."

Magnus Parador asked Carolus to lunch next day and Carolus drove over to find a long low secluded house with a beautifully kept garden. Magnus was short and voluble.

"My wife's in London for the day," he told Carolus. "So we shall be able to talk. I don't like discussing this in front of her. She was very fond of Felix and gets upset. Yes, your man Stick came over to see me. He was with my brother for some years before either of them got married. I don't think Felix committed suicide."

"So Stick says."

"It doesn't make sense, Deene. Happily married. No money worries. Easy conscience. A good brain in excellent condition. What would make him take his own life?"

"I've known a good many cases of suicide," said Carolus. "In very few of them could those who knew the man understand it."

"You accept the coroner's verdict, then?"

"I accept nothing. But I want something more to go on. I understand how you feel, of course. But there's only one possible alternative to suicide here."

"You mean, murder?"

"It couldn't have been an accident."

"I agree."

"And if it was murder you seem to be up against the why of it as much as with suicide. Had your brother any enemies?"

"My brother was in Far Eastern Intelligence before the war. Thank God the Japs never knew that. He was in one of their prisoner-of-war camps for two years. I gather the enmities made in those places are everlasting."

"I see. But you have never heard of anything of that kind in connection with your brother?"

"No. I'm bound to admit I haven't. Then there was his money. He was by any standards a very rich man. Where there is a lot of money there is some motive, I suppose."

21

"Only for those who will inherit it?"

Magnus smiled grimly.

"Meaning his wife and me? And Stick, of course."

"No one else?"

"Oh yes. Lots. Legacies which were not large for him but would mean a lot to the recipients. The vicar over there, man named Hopelady, would get a thousand or two—for his children, I think. My brother was godfather to one of them. His gardener, Boggett. His solicitor—and mine by the way—Graham Thriver. Old friend of ours. I don't know all his business affairs but he had invested some money in a big West End gun shop belonging to two brothers named Limpole. They all lived at Brenstead, by the way. Of course I'm not suggesting that any of them did him in for what he might inherit, but you asked about legacies."

Neither spoke for a few moments.

"I've only read a newspaper account of the inquest," said Carolus. "But there seems no doubt that he died of an overdose of Opilactic sleeping pills. Are you suggesting that he was forced to swallow these?"

"No. That's absurd. I don't know what happened. But there's something I don't like about it. I understand you're a bit of an expert on these things. Why don't you investigate? I'd be delighted to foot any bill you might want to submit."

"I never take on a case unless it interests me," said Carolus. "When it does, I don't want money. I enjoy it. You find that morbid, perhaps?"

"A little. But I hope this is going to interest you. Stick tells me you've cleared up a lot of very curious circumstances. There's one other thing here. My brother travelled with the same five men every day. They all tell a story about a man sitting in my brother's seat next morning and announcing rather impressively that he wouldn't be coming. That rouse your curiosity?"

"Did any of them know the man?"

"No. They all describe him but each paints a different picture, of course. Apparently he wore dark glasses during the whole journey. If you can't see a man's eyes you never know what he looks like. They differ about his height, his age and everything else. But they all think he knew something."

"Why didn't they ask him?"

"You know what commuters are like first thing in the morning. And of course they had no reason to think anything was amiss then. They just supposed Felix had missed his train. But in retrospect it does seem rather odd."

"Yes. But that, too, can be explained in many ways. Was there any evidence at the inquest to explain how he obtained the Opilactic?"

"No. But if my brother had wanted to obtain it he could, I daresay. It's sold abroad more freely than here. He spent a holiday in Tangier with Elspeth quite recently, for instance."

"Tell me about his wife, if you don't mind," said Carolus.

"I like her. Always have. Bit emotional. She'd been on the stage, I believe. I'd describe them as a devoted couple."

"Did you see much of them?"

"Not recently. I can't bear that place Brenstead. My father bought the manor house there many years ago, before anyone thought of making it a dormitory town. They left the house and most of the grounds alone and out of a sort of obstinacy Felix continued to live there when they built up all round him. But I found it oppressive. They didn't often come over here, either. But Felix and I met in town for lunch once a week."

"When did you see him last?"

"Three days before this happened."

"And you noticed nothing unusual?"

"Absolutely nothing. He seemed particularly cheerful, in fact. He was an easy-going fellow."

"You think, in other words, that in spite of the coroner's verdict, by some means that you cannot even guess, your brother was murdered?"

"Put like that it does sound a bit unlikely. I think there's some mystery about his death. That would be nearer to the mark. Or something may have happened suddenly to make him commit suicide. I don't know."

"He couldn't possibly have been the victim of a blackmailer?"

Magnus was silent.

" Unless there's a whole chapter of his life of which I know nothing I don't see how it's possible. He wasn't the sort of man a blackmailer would go for. And if he was he wouldn't have got out of it that way. He'd have told me for one thing."

" It's one possible explanation, though."

" I suppose so. The whole thing beats me. Let's go in to lunch."

The lunch was good but Carolus was not talkative. Just after they returned to the room in which they had sat before eating he said suddenly to Magnus, " Did your brother carry any sort of brief-case when he went to town?"

Magnus smiled.

" It's funny I never thought of that. Of course he did; I gave it him myself. There was no mention of it at the inquest so I suppose it wasn't found in the car."

" What kind of brief-case was it?"

" I'll show you in a minute because I've got its double. I bought them in Spain just over a year ago. Took my fancy, rather. Saw them in a shop-window in Madrid. They were dull red in colour, very soft Moroccan leather. I got one for myself and one to give Felix."

" He used it?"

" All the time. I used to see it every week when he came to lunch."

" He knew you had one like it?"

" No. I never told him. He was not keen, ever since childhood, on us having the same things. So I never took it with me when we met for lunch. Hang on a minute. You shall see it."

Magnus came back in a few minutes with a brief-case of dull crimson Moroccan leather, a thing of quality and distinction yet not outré or ostentatious.

" Felix's looked just like this when I saw it last. They'd worn about equally."

" Would you lend it me for a few days?"

" Certainly. If it will be of any help."

" I think it may. I'd like to see what reactions I get to it in Brenstead."

" Fair enough. I wonder what happened to Felix's, though. It could have been stolen after he was dead. By a chance passer-by, perhaps?"

" Was his wallet still on the body when they found him?"

" Yes. With seventy quid in it. And his watch. Nothing, the police said, had been disturbed."

Carolus thought for a moment. " I'll take this on, Parador," he said. " I'll go over to Brenstead tomorrow. I agree, there's something here that doesn't add up."

" I'm glad you'll take it."

" I think you had better let your solicitor know."

" Thriver? Yes, of course. You won't get much out of him. Cagey old character. He lives in Brenstead, I told you. I'll ring him up this evening. I'll also get in touch with the local doctor. Very good chap named Sporlott."

" And Mrs. Felix Parador."

" Yes. But don't upset her, will you? She's had a rough time through all this."

" I'll try not to. I shall have to see her, though. Is there anywhere to stay in Brenstead?"

" Yes. Quite a good pub. The landlord's a pain in the neck. One of these romancing types who has been everywhere and done everything. But the food's quite good, I believe. It's called the Royal Oak. You'll keep in touch, won't you?"

" Of course. Even if I find nothing questionable."

" Sure there's nothing else you want to ask me?"

" I don't think so. Unless there are any little personal details about your brother that might help."

" People found him reserved. He didn't chatter much. Some said he was mean. That was nonsense. He had his little economies like most rich men. He hated unnecessary phone calls and switched off lights whenever he saw them left on. But he could be absurdly generous."

" Did he drink much?"

" No. He liked a couple of stiff whiskies in the evening after a hard day, but I don't call that drinking. He was moderate in most things."

" Thanks," said Carolus. " I'll do what I can."

They parted with a handshake and Carolus drove his Bentley Continental with his usual caution towards Newminster. He put the car in the garage and reached his house as he had done on the day before, at tea-time.

Mrs. Stick made no reference to his journey but said severely, " The headmaster has been to see you, sir. He's coming back at five o'clock. I haven't told him . . . about Stick."

" No, of course not, Mrs. Stick."

When Mr. Gorringer returned to Carolus's study he seemed to be in the best of humour.

" Ah, Deene," he said. " I trust you will forgive this intrusion. I am aware that the holidays have begun and I am no longer in a position to demand your time. But I wanted a word with you."

Carolus, who knew only too well what ' a word ' might portend, said, " Certainly, headmaster. How about a drink?"

" It is barely five o'clock," said Mr. Gorringer. " But at your hospitable fireside who is to say no? Yes, a suspicion of whisky. I thank you. I came to ask if you have any special plans for the holidays?"

" Nothing fixed."

" My wife and I will make our customary sojourn in Ostende, of course, with occasional visits to the interesting old town of Bruges. But if you are remaining here I thought you might be attracted by the idea of a private pupil. With remuneration, I need hardly say."

" *Not* Priggley?"

" Your conjecture is correct. Rupert Priggley, a most difficult boy as I need scarcely remind you, has been left on our hands for the vacation. His father is once again in the salubrious American resort of Reno. His mother is on one of the Balearic Islands . . ."

" Ibiza, for certain."

" Again you are correct. They both have their private pre-occupations."

" Is that what you call them?"

"Let us not make mountains out of molehills. Some little matter of a divorce, I believe."

"The fourth. Yes. And the odious boy?"

"I will not conceal from you that I did my utmost to persuade him that he would be in a sane and suitable atmosphere with Hollingbourne who is taking his children to Eastbourne for a fortnight. But no. The young man in that impertinent way he has replied that it must be you or no one. It appears that he once had some experience with Hollingbourne's family which has prejudiced him."

"I know. Rounders on the sands. But I can't take him, headmaster. The responsibility is too great. Last time he produced a young woman whom he described as a piece of homework."

To the amazement of Carolus the headmaster thrust out his lips and made a man-of-the-world sound.

"Well, Deene, we were all boys once," he said. "I am particularly anxious that he should not be at a loose end in the town. It is apt to make people think that we do not have enough discipline over our pupils. He is a wayward boy, as you know."

"Wayward, you call it? He's a monster."

Carolus had not noticed that Mrs. Stick had entered behind him. He had often wondered at her weakness for the unspeakable Priggley.

"If you was thinking of me and Stick, sir," she said to Carolus, "I'm sure we could manage nicely. I've never known the young gentleman be any trouble to anyone. He's always behaved like a perfect gentleman."

"If that's your idea of a perfect gentleman I thank God I'm imperfect, Mrs. Stick," said Carolus harshly.

"I see I have our excellent Mrs. Stick on my side!" beamed Mr. Gorringer. "I may send Priggley round in the morning, then, Deene?"

"It's a disgraceful imposition," moaned Carolus.

"And I hope you have a very happy vacation," the headmaster added as he rose to go.

Ten minutes later there was a ring at the front door and Priggley himself entered.

27

" Aren't you ever going to be too old for The Queen's School?" asked Carolus miserably.

" I don't see why, sir. Billy Bunter was fifty-seven years at school."

" Oh, shut up. And leave that decanter alone. You're not getting whisky in this house."

" Not a teeny?"

" Not even what the headmaster calls a suspicion."

" Well, sir, what's on the *tapis*? Got a nice little crime up your sleeve for us?"

" There is a little matter I'm thinking of investigating," admitted Carolus.

" Goody. How many murders so far?"

" None, according to the coroner's verdict."

" That means we're right in," said Priggley who had managed to help himself to Carolus's Highland Malt. " Well, here's to it!" he added, raising his glass.

Chapter Three

During the long drive to Brenstead next morning Rupert Priggley was fairly subdued. Beyond offering to drive the Bentley two or three times, offering Carolus a box of Montecristo cigars which his father had smuggled in on his last visit and unwisely left at home, and suggesting various stops for what he described as nips, top-ups or quickies, he did not interfere with Carolus's thoughts. They reached the famous Dormitory town, 'the most remarkable display of domestic architecture in England since the war', it had been called, at about noon.

"God, how grim can they get?" asked Priggley.

It was at once obvious from the houses built that income brackets and status symbols had not been forgotten by the planners. There were houses with fair-sized gardens and garages and young trees yearning to shield them from view, small houses in long well-disciplined rows with small gardens and garages and, in the majority, houses without garages and gardens intended only for vegetables. There had been self-conscious attempts to avoid monotony so that some roads of houses curved gently, others were straight, some had rustic fences, some brick walls, some houses had little porches over their front doors, some were without. All was carefully graded according to income.

In the centre of the town were blocks of flats, each having its status. From one with a porter in uniform and a marble entry hall down to what were once called tenement buildings, they were carefully graded. Under them were shops which varied only in the goods they sold—size and window-space being identical.

It was all bright with pink bricks, lively paintwork, little squares of garden, scraps of modern statuary, a children's playground or two, several cinemas and a number of cafés. There were schools in allotted numbers and the original parish church of the village of Brenstead had been augmented with a thing that looked like a vast tortoise carrying a cross.

" Yes. It wouldn't be my choice of a place to live in," admitted Carolus, " but I can't see why life should be any less interesting here than elsewhere. Rows of identical houses don't make their inhabitants identical, as the Victorians found. Let's take a look at what is surely called ' the old part of the town '. Felix Parador had the original manor house."

They found a notice ' Manor Lane ' at the corner of a street of large villas set back from the road. On the same corner was a cottage, probably the original lodge-keeper's cottage of a large estate. They turned up this road and went for several hundred yards between gardens before they saw a small Georgian house on the right with ' The Old Manor ' on its gate.

" That's all I want to see," said Carolus. " Let's find The Royal Oak."

This had once been a modest inn, built at the same time as the manor house in the same direct four-square style of Georgian architecture, but it had been enlarged into a vast splaying hybrid building with a vivid sign in front of it, window-boxes now full of wallflowers and forget-me-nots, all with an appearance of self-conscious cheerfulness. Why didn't they buy an old coach and horses and drive the thing up to the doors every half-hour? Carolus wondered. Or at least get a man to lean against the wall smoking a churchwarden pipe? Or play a record of the merry laughter of serving wenches coming from the back yard?

" Frankly," said Priggley, " it makes me sick."

They found the bar which was exactly what they expected, electric lights in quaint old lanterns, chromes and horse-brasses, barrel-top seats and a man in an Old Etonian tie behind it.

" Ice?" said the man when he had poured Carolus's Scotch.

" No, thanks."

" I always ask," said the man in a voice which might have been polished up on a grindstone. " Never drink without it myself. Learnt that in the Andaman Islands. Chief Security Officer there for a couple of years at the end of the war. Nehru asked me to take it on after Independence but I had to refuse. They wanted me in Japan."

Rupert appeared to be lost in wonder for he had not been prepared for this.

" You like running this pub?" asked Carolus, trying to bring the conversation a little nearer home.

" So so. My name's Gray-Somerset, by the way."

" Deene," said Carolus.

" Yes, so so. I have my off days. The place is ghastly, of course. But I scarcely see it. Reminds me of Madegescar. Never left one's shack. I was out there crocodile hunting. Paying game that. Used to bring in ten or a dozen skins a day. Ever done any?"

" No," said Carolus. " You don't like Brenstead? Or is it the people?"

Gray-Somerset smiled indulgently.

" Well, they're obviously not my sort . . ."

" No?"

" Well, obviously not."

" You mean they don't come in here?"

" Oh, I can't complain of the business. Nor can the brewers. An uncle of mine has some shares in this outfit. Lord Plumstead, as a matter of fact. No, *business* is all right. I meant the people."

" What about them?"

" Well, I mean the type. Obviously not *me*."

" Cliquish?"

" It's not so much that. I mean there's no one here, when you come to think of it. Not a soul."

Carolus persisted in misunderstanding.

"Yes. You are a bit quiet today," he said looking round him. "Perhaps it's the result of the inquest you had the other day."

Gray-Somerset looked superior.

"S'metter of fact," he said, "we've been rather busier since then. Better sort of local people."

"Oh. There are grades?"

"Certainly. Man named Thriver, for instance . . ."

"Who's he?"

"Solicitor. Big practice in Pell Mell. Came in on the very night Parador killed himself. Never been in before but comes quite often now."

"The very night, eh?" said Carolus, acting dumb. "Strange that. What time?"

"Just before closing time."

"Perhaps he was Parador's solicitor?"

"He was. But what's that to do with his coming in here?"

"See your point," said Carolus. "Would you put him in Grade One?"

"Definitely," said Gray-Somerset. "Better type than most of them. His brother and I did the Schönspitz together. Hell of a climb that was."

"Who else of that grade comes in?"

Gray-Somerset remained quite serious.

"Man called Dogman. Useful character if you're a betting man. I don't follow the gees as I used to. Never go for long chances, anyway. No, a gran at evens is my form and only now and again."

"Dogman lives here?"

"Yes. Just round the corner in Manor Lane. Most of the better types live up there. He was in that night, too. Telling me about some shooting he'd done. Got a panther it seems. Took him upstairs and showed him my skins. Three tigers. I was only in Assam three weeks."

"I suppose he stayed till closing-time, too?"

"No. S'metter of fect he didn't. Went off about nine-thirty. I noticed because I went out to see if the sign was on. That half-wit Hopelady told me it was out. His idea of a joke, I suppose. I saw Dogman drive away."

" Towards his home?"

" No. Opposite direction. On the Great Ring road."

It did not seem to occur to Mr. Gray-Somerset to ask Carolus why he should be interested enough to ask questions about the movements of certain people on a certain night. He was too obsessed with his own affairs.

" It was a pitch black night, I remember. Not a sign of a moon . . ."

" Been there, too?" asked Carolus.

" S'funny you should ask that. The Americans wanted me at Cape Kennedy some years ago. They knew my parachute record."

" I think I'll have another Scotch," said Carolus. " You wouldn't have a couple of vacant rooms for a few nights, would you?"

" Perhaps you'd ask the booking-clerk in the hall, would you? I try not to interfere with his arrangements."

" What about some lunch?" asked Carolus.

" The head-waiter will tell you about that. He was the steward on a yacht I had once. Took her round the Horn in '62."

Carolus was amused to notice that Priggley did not think the Munchausen character of Mr. Gray-Somerset was worth commenting on. His manner said all too clearly that he had known this sort of thing before.

Just then there was a disturbance from behind the partition which separated them from the private bar. Voices were raised in astonishment and one voice, that of an old man, could be heard giving an explanation.

Mr. Gray-Somerset, who could see what was going on, interpreted to Carolus.

" One of our local characters, an old man named Gobler, seems to have been badly smashed up. Go through and hear about it if you're interested."

In the public bar Carolus found a group round an ancient

character whose head was bandaged. He was sitting leaning on a heavy stick.

"Yes, the doctor said I wasn't to drink anything, but I thought to myself, one pint wouldn't do any harm so I came round here."

No one else seemed to catch the delicate nuances in this appeal and Carolus quietly responded to it, placing a glass mug before Mr. Gobler.

"Thank you, sir," he said casually, and continued his narrative. "Must have been about eight o'clock," he said. "I was on my way round here at the time."

"Thought it was funny your not coming in last night," said someone.

"How could I? It was all I could manage to get back home and send my daughter for the doctor. You try being knocked over by a car and see how you like it."

"Where did it happen?"

"Down the bottom of Manor Lane as they call it now." He turned to Carolus. "Used to be the entrance to the Park," he explained. "They've turned it into a road now. Where all the big houses are. Coming from my place I had to cross the end of it, if you see what I mean. It takes me quite a bit of time to go that distance."

"He's not very sure on his pins, the old chap," explained the man next to Carolus, *sotto voce.*

"I must have been about half-way across when I see this car coming full at me out of the Lane."

"What kind of car?"

Gobler stopped his narrative and looked up shrewdly at his interrogator.

"You ask me what *kind* of a car? There's a bloody silly question for you. How am I to know what kind of a car it was? All I see was the lights coming at me."

"But didn't it stop afterwards?"

"If you'll wait a minute I'll tell you what it did. Here's your good health. sir." Mr. Gobler paused to drink and lowered the level of his beer by some two inches. "As I was saying, I see these lights coming at me. So what did I do?"

" Got out of the way pretty bloody quick, if you had any sense," said one of the audience.

" You can talk," allowed Gobler. " It's easy to say that. But how could I? I can't stump along any quicker than I do. I tried to go one way and the car seemed to swerve as though it had only just seen me and I found myself flat on my back. Just as though someone had given me a hell of a kick up the arse, if you'll excuse the expression."

" What about the car then?"

" It seemed to slow up a bit and I started giving 'em hell. ' You lousy bastard!' I shouted out. ' What you think you're up to?' At that he just drives on fast as he could."

" Must have known you were all right from you swearing like that."

" But I wasn't all right. The back of my head was bursting open. I could feel the blood down my neck. It took me I don't know how long to get to my feet. I don't suppose I'll ever be able to walk again."

There were two replies to this from the audience, neither of them very sympathetic.

" Well, you couldn't walk much before, could you?"

" You got here all right this morning."

Gobler ignored this.

" You should have heard what the doctor said. I've got a contusion, he told my daughter. It's the next best thing to a concussion as far as I can make out. What do you say about that?"

" You wouldn't be here if there was anything wrong with you. Still, the bloke in the car ought to have stopped."

" 'Course he ought."

" It's not right. Who d'you think it was, Gobler?"

" I haven't any idea. He didn't stop for me to ask."

" Looks like it was someone belonging to the place. Coming out of Manor Lane at eight o'clock in the evening."

" Is Manor Lane a cul-de-sac?" asked Carolus.

" It doesn't lead to anywhere," he was told. " There's a couple of houses beyond the Manor and that's all."

" Could have been someone who'd been calling on one of the

houses in the Lane. Sure it wasn't a delivery van, Gobler?"

" No. It wasn't a van. I could see that."

"What colour was it?"

" That's what the policeman asked me. Came round this morning. I said to him, ' how d'you expect me to say what colour it was? I was flat out on my back at the time.' He started to get on his high horse then. ' All right,' I said, ' you tell me what colour it was. You're the police, aren't you?' D'you know what he said then? I should have noticed the number! Did you ever hear anything so bloody silly in your life?"

The recital was interrupted by the entrance from the saloon bar of a sturdy intelligent-looking man in his forties. It soon became apparent that this was a doctor.

" Come on, Gobler," he said in a friendly way. " I'm going to give you a lift home. I told you to lie up for a few days."

" I was just telling them what you said, doctor. I've got contusion."

" You'll have worse than that if you go running about the place. Now come on, you old sinner."

While Gobler was finishing his pint, Carolus asked the doctor if his name was Sporlott and hearing that it was told him who he was.

" Oh, yes. Magnus Parador phoned me. Like to come in for a drink this evening? About nine?"

" Thanks."

Carolus and Priggley reached the dining-room just in time.

" Another ten minutes and you'd have had it," said a very superior head-waiter regretfully.

" Why were you so interested in the ancient mariner with the bruised bottom?" asked Priggley.

" Because the car didn't stop."

" Lots of cars don't stop after accidents."

" Not in circumstances like that. It must have been travelling very slowly. Perhaps with sidelights only. When the driver saw the old fellow he braked and swerved of course, and by the time he hit him he had almost stopped, otherwise the old man wouldn't be alive now. He heard Gobler swearing, so knew there couldn't be much wrong. *Any* driver, unless he had some very good reason not to, would have stopped. Drivers know what a chance they take by not stopping after an accident. It automatically makes them to blame. Yet this one drove on."

"I see your point," said Priggley. "Gobler said he'd nearly crossed so it must have been the onside bumper that hit him. Think the police will find the car?"

"Could be. But it may not have dented the bumper at all."

"If so, what will happen to the chap who was driving?"

Carolus looked steadily at Priggley.

"Why ' the chap' who was driving? What makes you so sure it was a man?"

"Gobler said . . ."

"No, he didn't. He assumed as you did that it was a man. He never even saw the driver."

"That's true. What do we do this afternoon. Wait. Give me three guesses. Interview a suspect?"

"There aren't any. There isn't even a crime."

"But there damn soon will be with you around."

"We go to have a look at this landmark they call The Great Ring. That's where the body, the only body we've got, was found."

Carolus had no difficulty, after lunch, in booking two rooms for the night. After Priggley had brought their suitcases in they set off.

The Great Ring lay half-way between Brenstead and Buttsfield, another great dormitory town being built to out-match Brenstead in population. The distances were approximately equal, ten miles from Buttsfield to The Great Ring and between ten and eleven from The Great Ring to Brenstead.

Carolus passed The Three Thistles Inn and thought its closed doors had a slightly self-righteous look at three o'clock in the afternoon as though saying ' *we* would never let anyone in After Hours. You know *us*.' He took the narrower road to the left at a National Monuments sign indicating that it led to The Great Ring. He went up an incline to the car park and found about a dozen cars there.

Even from here there was a stupendous view of the country-side, broken as it was by tree-tops.

"Let's see the thing itself," said Carolus.

It had all been laid out by the County or the Rural District or Arts Council, or the National Trust or someone, neat little concrete steps with a hand-rail and iron seats every twenty steps.

"I wonder if that shocker behind the bar has climbed this one," said Priggley as they reached the last flight of steps.

The Ring itself was disappointing, a circle of stones no taller than a man among which the occupants of the cars parked below wandered admiringly like people at an exhibition of modern sculpture.

"Ever so heavy they must have been to bring right up here," remarked a large woman stertorously.

"I expect they knew what they were doing," said her comfortable companion.

"Must of," said the first.

Rupert Priggley had gone outside the circle and was looking at the astonishingly vast stretch of country beneath them.

"There is something odd about this place, sir," he said. "But I'll tell you something—I had the same feeling in Brenstead itself today."

"What on earth do you mean?"

"I don't quite know. All those ghastly houses. People trying to perpetuate themselves by building. It's all so futile."

"I shouldn't call those stones futile."

"What? I suppose they were intended for some kind of worship. Look at them now. I don't know quite what I do mean."

"I agree there's something almost macabre about Brenstead. Forty-thousand dwelling-places built in a few years and packed tight like a honeycomb. A lot more eerie than this. I could believe in anything happening there. You don't make people conform to a pattern by putting them in uniform houses. Outwardly, perhaps, but only outwardly. I think we're going to find some very odd things in Brenstead since you mention oddity."

"Behind those tidy house-fronts?" grinned Rupert.

"Exactly," said Carolus and they returned to the car.

38

Chapter Four

WHEN HE REACHED THE HOTEL CAROLUS TELEPHONED TO THRIVER and was surprised to find the solicitor wanted to see him as soon as possible. He had anticipated difficulty in seeing him at all, in spite of Magnus's introduction.

" Come round at once, if you like," Thriver said in his rather high-pitched voice. " We live in Lower Manor Lane. Take no notice of any name you may see on the gate. It's number 12."

Priggley stared at the crimson brief-case which Carolus carried when he prepared to set out.

"What's that for?" he asked. But without waiting for an answer, said, " I'm going to have a cruise round the town. See you at breakfast."

" Don't . . ." began Carolus but stopped. What was the good?

He found out why he was to ignore anything but the number on Thriver's mock-Elizabethan villa. Some previous owner had called it Kumyu-in.

The lawyer came to the door himself and showed Carolus into a room like a law office. Thriver was a rat-like man, shifty-eyed and sharp-featured. Rat-like was so very much the word that

Carolus was fascinated to think his squeaky voice rat-like, even his little white claw-like hands. His mouth, too, thin-lipped and toothy had a gnawing look about it.

"Whisky or brandy?" he asked without preamble in a sharp, business-like way.

Carolus told him.

"I'm glad you've come. I've been trying to get Magnus over, but he's a lazy fellow. I'm in some difficulty."

This was the first time he had heard a solicitor make any such admission, Carolus thought.

"I know all about you," Thriver continued. "And you have full authority from Magnus. So I shan't beat about the bush. On the very day of his death—if he died before midnight, that is—Felix came to my office and put his signature to a new will I had drawn up for him and took it away with him."

"In his pocket?"

"No. In a . . . Why that's the very brief-case!"

"I'm afraid not. It's the twin. Magnus Parador lent it to me. He bought two originally and gave one to Felix."

"I see. I thought I recognised it. I wish it were, because it would mean that the will had been found."

"Felix had made a will before the one he signed that day?"

"Oh, several. He had a rich man's privilege of changing his mind."

"Were the provisions of the new one very much changed?"

"Not the basic provisions. The bulk of his fortune still went to his wife and brother. They were not affected. But some of the smaller legacies, if you call five thousand pounds a small legacy, were . . . well, two were cut out altogether."

"Yes?"

"I tried to dissuade Felix. It seemed so unlike him to avenge two paltry quarrels. But he did not like his word disputed, you know. In many ways a very obstinate man. He could be generous, yes, but he could also be petty. He cut out Dr. Sporlott because of an argument they had. Sporlott openly laughed at his views, I believe. The other was Hopelady. He was godfather to one of Hopelady's five children. A boy named Matthew. He had left a

40

large sum to Hopelady for this boy's benefit but he put it out of the father's reach. The boy was to inherit it when he was twenty-two unless it could be shown that he had in any way anticipated his inheritance."

" I see. Were those the only two unlucky ones, the doctor and the vicar?"

" Yes."

" Any new beneficiaries?"

" Yes. That's the point. That's where the difficulty arises. A woman named Henrietta Ballard. An actress, I understand, whom he had met through his wife. He had been . . . maintaining her for three years. He had bought her a house at Buttsfield, about twenty miles away. He left her a thousand a year for life. That was why his will was such a secret. No one was to know of this, least of all Elspeth. That's understandable, of course."

" Oh quite. And no one does know?"

" No one. My confidential clerk who has been with me twenty years, an entirely dependable man who knows none of the people concerned and cares less, typed it. Otherwise no one knows that it was ever made."

" Unless Parador told anyone."

" It's scarcely likely, is it?"

" He might have told the girl Henrietta Ballard that he was going to look after her."

" She's been abroad for two months. Comes back tomorrow, I believe."

" It's not impossible, though."

" Very unlikely. Felix specifically told me that no one knew what he was doing."

" Who witnessed his signature?"

" My confidential clerk. Felix had known him for years. Old Tasman is a very proper old chap and Felix pulled his leg. That afternoon he pulled out his pocket flask of whisky and poured out two measures. Old Tasman had to drink one—he knows I never drink in the office. It emptied his flask, and Tasman was quite flushed up. But as for him repeating anything he learned in the office—impossible! Quite impossible!"

41

" I see."

" The question is, where is this will now?"

" If Parador committed suicide . . ."

" Of course he did."

" You are sure of that, Mr. Thriver?"

" Absolutely. I know what made him do it. He was convinced he had cancer. That was the cause of his quarrel with Sporlott. Some charlatan of a foreign doctor told him so a year ago."

" Had he any symptoms?"

" I understand he suffered from digestive troubles, chest pains, heartburn and so on. I haven't discussed it with Sportlott. But people have killed themselves before now by making themselves believe they have cancer. He killed himself because of it."

" You sound very positive. Perhaps you know why he chose that particular time and place?"

" His choice of time I understand. He was only waiting to sign his will. I told you he was both a generous and a vindictive man. He wanted to look after his mistress. And I'm afraid he also wanted to make sure the two men who had angered him did not benefit."

" Yet he was so careless about the will that he kept it with him and left it either in his pocket or his dispatch-case when he took his overdose?"

" Probably the risk never occurred to him."

" You also know his reason for choosing the place?"

" Oh yes. That's quite plain. You must remember that his family and mine lived here before Brenstead became a dormitory town. We used to cycle out to The Great Ring as boys. It was a favourite picnic place for us before it became a tourist stop. A few people came to see it in those days, but very few. Poor Felix was simply returning, as so many men do in a time of crisis, to his boyhood."

" I don't say you're wrong," said Carolus, " but it's all a bit too neat and tied up and tidy for me. Of course I didn't know Parador. But Magnus tells me he was very fond of his wife. Wouldn't he have wanted to save her feelings?"

42

" So far as possible, he did. She has told me how he rang her up that afternoon to say he wasn't coming home. He meant the first news she would have of it to come when the body was found. It was the best he could do."

" I see what you mean. I still don't like it, though."

Thriver seemed to become a little rambling.

" I've known the brothers Parador since boyhood. We grew up together, in fact. I'm by no means a sentimental or a superstitious man, but I have certain presentiments. I *knew* that evening there was something wrong."

" Had there been anything to notice about Felix's manner that afternoon?"

" No. No. He was quite himself—cheerful, in fact. It wasn't that. It was a presentiment. I felt it so strongly that during the evening I decided to go round to see him. I got out the car and drove round."

" Yes?"

" I could hear the noise from a television set as I stood at the front door. Elspeth opened it and I asked for Felix. 'Didn't you know?' she said. 'He's not coming down tonight. He phoned me.' I was surprised that she didn't ask me in, but she said she was going to bed as soon as that particular television programme ended."

" *She* had no presentiment, anyway."

" No, poor girl. She was quite bright. Then I did an unusual thing. I decided to call at The Royal Oak for a drink. That made Elspeth laugh. '*You* going to The Oak?' she said. 'I've a good mind to come with you.' I said, 'Why don't you?' But she was tired and I went alone."

" Who was there? At The Royal Oak, I mean?"

" Dogman. No one else whom I recognised. But after a little time Rumble came in. You'll meet him. Quiet fellow. Lives here in Lower Manor Road. The next house down. It's quite a small place but Rumble wasn't well off when he first came. Used to run about on a motor-cycle. Then his wife died and he inherited a little which he put into a travel agency. He's doing quite well now. Travels up with us every day."

" You were in the railway carriage when this unknown man got in next morning? What was your impression?"

" Not much at the time. You see I knew that Felix wouldn't be coming because Elspeth had told me he was staying in town, but I said nothing to the others. I wondered how this man should know, but that's all. It was only when I knew Felix was dead I thought there was something suspicious about it."

" But not enough to make you change your opinion that it was suicide?"

" Oh no, I was sure of that, and I am still. Let me give you another drink."

" It's strange to me that you and Magnus, who are the two men who apparently knew Felix best, hold exactly opposite opinions about that."

" So I gather. Magnus can't believe it. He wants you to dig something up to upset the coroner's verdict. Well, Deene, I want you to find that will, if it still exists. Meanwhile come through and meet my wife and daughter."

Enid Thriver was looking for her spectacles. She was a large, untidy woman of indeterminate outline.

" How d'you do? I know I put them down here," she said. " Do sit down if the cats have left you a chair. You must have moved them, Patsy, darling. This is my daughter, Mr. . . . you didn't tell me his name, Graham. Deene, that's it. I can't see a thing without them."

Patsy was a brisk, square-shouldered girl who would have been attractive but for a slight squint and a downright manner.

" Hullo," she said. " I've read about you, of course. I wonder what you'll unearth in this little community? All sorts of horrors, I suppose."

" He must come along to Chatty Dogman's party next week," said Enid Thriver.

" Oh mums, you know it's tomorrow, not next week."

" Is it? I didn't know. I think you must be sitting on them, Patsy. No, here they are. I remember now. I put them between the pages of my book so that I shouldn't forget where I put them. Yes, Chatty's party. You'll meet a lot of people there. Elspeth's coming. She says Felix wouldn't have wanted her to mope for ever. Would you like some coffee, Mr. Deene? I'm dying to make some, if you would."

"Yes, I would indeed," said Carolus, who wanted Patsy to talk.

When Enid had left them, he asked her what she thought about Parador's death.

"I suppose it must have been suicide," she said. "But I can't see it. I was working with him on his memoirs, you know. Chiefly at week-ends."

"Were you? I didn't know that."

"Fascinating, yes. He's had a very interesting life. It's all in the Far East, though. Nothing about Brenstead."

"Not about his boyhood here?"

"No. They weren't that sort of memoirs, thank God. How bored I am with people's boyhoods and girlhoods. These started when he first went out to Shanghai before the war."

"Had he got far?"

"I'd typed about a hundred pages, but it was only provisional, he said. He had a lot of notes of the next part. Whether it would have ended up here or not I don't know."

"He gave you no idea of what was to come?"

"Not much. He was cagey about that."

"Did he mention the name of anyone you know?"

"No. Not even Magnus or Daddy."

"What did you know about this, Mr. Thriver?"

"Very little. As Patsy says, he was cagey. I believe he only meant to write about his M.I. experiences and perhaps his imprisonment."

Enid returned with a tray.

"Oh, Patsy, I've forgotten the sugar. I put it out ready, too. Darling, the little crystals. In the silver jug."

"Sure you've got the coffee?" asked Patsy getting up.

"Don't be silly, darling."

Carolus watched Enid pouring out. She could be proficient when she liked, he noticed. And there was a sharp intelligent expression on her face when she made her next remark.

45

" Graham won't tell us whether *we* get anything from Felix's will," she said. " You'd think so, when he left money to quite new people like Mr. Hopelady."

" Don't go into that now, dear," said Thriver in his high-pitched voice, but rather sharply.

" It's annoying, though," said Enid, and looked annoyed, too. " He *was* so enormously rich."

" You don't *know* that, Enid. I'd much rather you didn't discuss it."

Patsy returned.

" You left the gas on," she remarked as she put down a small china sugar bowl.

" Where are you staying?" Enid asked Carolus. " Not that dreadful Royal Oak?"

" It seems quite comfortable."

" I suppose it's better than the Rippinghurst. That's our new hotel. It's quite near here. Felix used to call this part of the town the Cantonment. It has been left more or less as it was, you see. Our house and the one next door are the only ones in this road from before the Dormitory Plan, but Manor Road is almost untouched. We're the last outposts."

" She means of the *ancien régime*," said Patsy. " After us the deluge—of bright new villas."

" Who lives in the other old house in this road?"

" Mr. Rumble. He lost his wife a couple of years ago and lives quite alone now. You must meet him."

" So your husband says."

" He'll be at Chatty's on Sunday."

" Tomorrow, darling," said Patsy.

" Oh yes, tomorrow. He's a good next-door-neighbour. Never a sound. Some more tea?"

" It's coffee, mums."

" No more, thank you, Mrs. Thriver. I promised to call in and see the doctor this evening."

" I'll phone Chatty and tell her to ask you. She'll be delighted to have another man. Didn't someone tell me you have your son with you?"

46

"My *son*? No, I've been spared that. My least favourite pupil has been wished on me for the holidays. But we only arrived to-day at lunch-time."

Carolus thought Enid Thriver looked far less vague as she said, "I know. Things get around very quickly in Brenstead. I must make sure Chatty asks him, too."

"Not if any respectable young girls are going to be there."

"Like that? You've been warned, Patsy. Elspeth Parador has a niece staying with her, I believe. She naturally doesn't want to be alone . . ."

Then quite suddenly the pleasant tranquility of the room was split open. Patsy, the downright Patsy, let out an ear-splitting shriek. Thriver was on his feet at once and Enid rushed over to her daughter.

"Patsy . . . darling . . ."

"What on earth?"

Carolus watched the three of them closely.

It was thirty seconds before Patsy was able to speak and when she did so only one word came from her.

"There!" she said, and pointed towards the uncurtained window.

It was enough for Carolus who did not waste time in going over to the window, but dashed into the hall and made for the front door. Even so, he was too late. As he ran across the round lawn towards the gates he heard, from the main road ten yards away, the sound of a motor-cycle starting with the first kick. He did not pause but ran to the corner. No use. He was in time to see a motor-bicycle without lights disappear. Just before it went out of sight its rider, as if derisively, switched on his lights, but the number plate was invisible.

He returned to the house to find Patsy in control of herself.

"I'd like a drink, please," she said to her father.

"He's gone," Carolus told her. "Off on a motor-bike before I could get a glimpse of him. What exactly did you see?"

"A face," said Patsy succinctly. "Nothing more, really. But he was wearing dark glasses. I've always had a fear since childhood of looking at a window at night and seeing a face outside."

47

"You're not the only one," said Carolus. "It's quite a common fear."

"I forgot to draw the curtains," said Enid.

"Absurd to get hysterical, I know," Patsy admitted, regaining her downright manner. "But it *was* rather beastly."

"Obviously you wouldn't be able to recognise the face again," Carolus suggested.

"Shouldn't think so. I had the impression that it was a youngish man, but that's all."

"Were they dark spectacles he was wearing? Or goggles?"

"Spectacles. I'm sure of that."

"What's under the window?" asked Carolus, walking towards it.

"Grass. I hate flower-beds against the house."

"I'm not going to look for footprints," said Carolus. "I leave that to the police. You're going to inform them, I suppose?"

"Certainly," said Thriver. "I don't want any more of this."

"They'll send round a Detective-Constable who'll take a lot of measurements and that'll be the last you hear of it."

Thriver turned on him, as though he did not want to hear the police slighted.

"I suppose you know who it was?" he asked.

"I don't know the name," admitted Carolus.

"Or why he should be looking in *my* windows."

"I think I know that," said Carolus.

This seemed to annoy Thriver, who went stiffly across to the telephone. But before he lifted the receiver he looked up at Carolus.

"If you know so much perhaps you can tell me whether this will happen again?"

"No. I don't think it will," said Carolus at once.

Thriver addressed himself to the telephone. In giving a curt and businesslike account of the occurrence he seemed to regain his good humour.

"Well, police or not," he said, "I want another drink and I'm sure you do, Deene. I heard you sprinting up the road. Sit down for a moment and let Sporlott wait."

When they were once again in his study with glasses in their hands, Thriver said confidentially, " Look here, Deene, you may as well tell me. Do you think what occurred tonight had anything to do with Parador's death?"

" I don't want to say too much. I've no real idea of anything yet. But by one line of supposition, still very vague, I think it might have, yes. In a very indirect way."

" If that's not caginess I don't know what is."

Carolus smiled.

" I always start with guessing," he said. " And my initial guesses are quite often wrong."

Perhaps Thriver was not accustomed to a third whisky for he seemed to grow quite facetious.

" Turn your crystal ball again," he said, " and look into the past. Do you see a murder?"

" I see one in the future," said Carolus and left it at that.

Chapter Five

CAROLUS FOUND DR. SPORLOTT'S HOUSE AND SURGERY IN THE centre of the new town. Cotswold stone had been cemented (a crime in itself) to make low walls round a piece of modern sculpture called Resurrection which looked like a tree struck by lightning. A square from which traffic was banned was called The Piazza, and a notice-board read, ' To the Tiny Tots' Playground : Qualified Nanny in Charge During Shopping Hours '. Another building had forthright class-free signs, ' Men ' and ' Women '. There was no one in sight as Carolus rang Sporlott's doorbell at nine o'clock.

A woman in a fur coat opened the door.

" Oh, you want Roger. I'm just off to play bridge. ROGER! Here's your visitor! Good night," she said briskly, and stepped out into The Piazza.

Sporlott came forward.

" Do come in. Sorry the wife had to go out. Bridge mad. I'm glad you managed to come. Magnus phoned me about you. Sit down," he said, and after offering Carolus a cigarette lit one himself. Carolus decided to play this one with reserve. He put the red brief-case beside him but it did not attract any attention.

"I had to get that old villain Gobler home this morning. There's not much wrong with him but he lost a little blood last night. He's seventy-odd and would have sat there while anyone bought drinks for him. He's known as a terrible old scrounger chiefly because he's really got the money to pay for his beer."

"What do you think happened?"

"A car must have been coming out of Manor Road without headlights, I suppose. The driver saw him all right and pulled up, but not quite soon enough. Its bumper must have caught the old boy behind the knees I should think, quite gently but enough to topple him over. He caught his head on something hard. But no bones broken. I can't think why the driver didn't stop." Sporlott grinned. "Interested in that, too?"

"I'm interested in anything that goes on here at the moment."

"Then you should come to this part of the town. Things happening all the time. These are the real people—not those status symbolists round the Manor."

"I can never quite understand why people who live in cheap houses in rows are supposed to be more *real* than any others."

Sporlott laughed.

"I used the wrong word, perhaps. You're interested in Parador's suicide, I understand."

"If it was suicide."

"I'm afraid it was. He was sure he had cancer."

"And had he?"

"Not according to every test we can apply. He had what one might call malignant gastritis. Result of semi-starvation in a Japanese prisoner-of-war camp. But you couldn't tell him that. We fell out over it. Terrible row, we had. We haven't spoken for six months. Pity, because I liked him and his wife. But this was an obsession."

"He wasn't a man to quarrel with, I gather."

"Oh, I don't know. He may have been vindictive in some cases. He just shut me out."

"Unforgiving, though? If he had meant to leave you anything

51

in his will, do you think he'd have cut you out?"

Sporlott considered this.

"He wouldn't have left me anything in the first place. He had no reason to. But if he had—yes, I suppose he'd have changed it."

"He was a private patient of yours?"

"Yes. He went to a colleague of mine after our row. Very good chap, Indian, Kumar Shant. Over at Buttsfield. He's managed, so far, to keep clear of the cancer issue. I see Elspeth from time to time and she tells me all about it. Parador's been suffering from heartburn and Kumar has just recently prescribed Buscapine. I don't know whether he had started taking it. Perfectly harmless, anyway."

"What about sleeping pills?"

"Never took any. Had a thing against them. 'Take one of those,' he once told me, 'and you've formed a habit'."

"You never prescribed Opilactic for him then?"

"Certainly not. I'm against using antibiotics except in cases of real necessity."

"I noticed Opilactic in the medicine cupboard in Thriver's bathroom tonight."

"Really? I'm not surprised. Thriver has a most morbid interest in drugs and ailments."

"You don't think you prescribed them?"

"It's possible. I do seem to remember his complaining of insomnia a year or so ago."

"These were supplied by Scotter, a local chemist."

"Then I must have prescribed them. Scotter's a stickler for prescriptions."

"Where do you think Parador got his?"

"Abroad, very likely. Perhaps he bought it in readiness. You'd be surprised to know how many people walk about with a means to end life handy."

"So you have confidence in Scotter?"

"Absolutely. Painfully conscientious. He's a pompous stick, terribly class conscious and all that, but knows his job and sticks to the rules. You'll find him that not so rare thing, a Socialist snob. Very defiantly as-good-as-you-are, against all class barriers, but can't help name-dropping and terribly pleased when he's asked somewhere to play bridge. Know the type?"

"Yes. But I want to meet this example of it."

Carolus stood up. He felt vaguely unsatisfied as though Sporlott could have told him, without breach of professional confidence, a good deal more than he had chosen to, in spite of his frank manner.

"One piece of advice I'd like to give you," said Sporlott as Carolus pulled on his coat. "Don't concentrate too much on the people in the villas. You'll hear a lot more from the remnants of the old working people. Not from my patients, the real workers, they don't give a damn who swallowed what. But from the few who are stranded in the old town. There's a man named Boggett, for instance, who worked for Parador. I bet he knows more than all the ladies and gentlemen of the place put together. They're not with it, Deene. They still think I'm going to call on them in a brougham. People like Boggett talk and hear and remember. Moreover they see."

As this was the advice which Carolus had been following all his professional life and intended to follow here, he was not profuse in his thanks.

He reached The Royal Oak to find Priggley ' having a nightcap' in the public bar. Before he could protest Priggley put a whisky in front of him with exactly the right amount of soda, and smiled affably.

"There's quite a lot *about*," Priggley said, as though there was no doubt about Carolus's interest in his achievements. "But it all seems rather tied up, if you know what I mean. Time will tell. How did you get on?"

"Tolerably."

"There's a character here named Boggett you should meet. He worked for Parador—at least he was employed by him. Gingerhaired. Boozy. Never stops talking, chiefly about which he's got his eye on and what he could do with that one."

"I've heard about him, but not of the amorous side of his character which you artlessly convey. It's too late to tackle him

53

now, I think. He'll keep, anyway. I've done quite enough in ten hours."

But Boggett had other ideas. He lurched across in a sidelong way, his little red-rimmed eyes looking in no particular direction, and addressed Carolus.

" I been talking to your son," he announced in a husky voice.

" This," said Carolus with some asperity, " is *not* my son."

" No. Didn't think he was," said Boggett quickly. " He's all there, though. No flies on him, as you might say. He knows what he's doing. Know what he told me he's been up to this evening?"

" I'll believe anything," sighed Carolus.

" Least said soonest mended," agreed Boggett. " I'm not the one to tell tales out of school. I like a bit of what's-it myself. I'm no spoil-sport. See that one standing over there with no stockings on and her hair in a knot? I could do with a bit of that. Yes. I wouldn't mind that in front of a nice warm fire. That would be all right, that would."

" You worked for Mr. Felix Parador, I believe?" said Carolus to cut short these reflections.

Boggett's eyes and mind were brought into focus.

" Certainly I did. I was his head gardener for a good many years, and a better gentleman I couldn't wish to meet. I can't say the same of Ur, though. If I was to tell you . . ."

" Why don't you?"

" Wouldn't do. Not if you knew all I know. I don't say there was anything in it, mind you. You mustn't only think the worst of people. But what I've seen in the day-time's enough, never mind what went on at night when I wasn't there."

" What sort of thing?"

" Nothing that you could really say anything about whatever you might think. But it doesn't always mean because a man's a parson and preaching about temptation in the church on Sunday he's any better than anyone else. Does it? I can't see why it should take him a couple of hours to ask for a subscription. I'd give him Hopelady. Then what about that Rumble? Quiet sort of fellow he is. But I know some of these quiet ones. He doesn't go to her now because she's got her young niece there staying with

54

her but that's not to say she doesn't go to him, with him all alone in the house. See what I mean? Nor I wouldn't put Thriver above it."

" Above what?"

" What I'm talking about. I wouldn't trust him further than I could see him, not with her about."

Carolus began to wonder where this scandalous catalogue would end.

" You wouldn't think anything of those Limpoles, would you? Chapel and that. But I've seen the younger one go off in the car with her or may I be struck dead. Makes you think, doesn't it?"

" No," said Carolus. " Where were you the night Mr. Parador died, Boggett?"

" Where was I? Why in here, of course, till closing time."

" What was closing time that night?"

" Half past ten. This silly bee always packs up right on the dot. It's no good asking for another. Time gentlemen, please, he says and it is time. What do you think of that?"

" Did you go straight home?"

" Well, I may have larked about a little time. There was a party in here that night . . ."

" A party?"

" I mean a young woman who was staying with her sister and had to get home in case they locked her out. But I was in by eleven o'clock. I live just along at the corner."

" Were you disturbed that night at all?"

" It's a funny thing you should ask me that. I told several about it but the police never asked me anything. Soon after I got in I heard two cars go by, coming out of Manor Lane. There's not much traffic at that time and I couldn't help wondering. They seemed to be following one another. They both turned round into the main road and went off."

" In which direction?"

" Buttsfield way. The wife was in bed and snoring like an old hippo but I didn't seem to be able to get to sleep that night. I must have dozed off because I was woken up a couple of hours later, or that's what it seemed, by a noise of car engines again, or at least that's what I thought it was."

"Don't you get traffic along that main road at night?"

"Very little. It's cross-country like. The London road's over the other side of the town. Anyway, there's traffic that wakes you up and traffic that doesn't. This did and it may be because I was thinking of the other, the two cars that came out of Manor Lane. Only this was different. It was one car and a motor-bike. First the car, then after a little bit the motor-bike. They both turned into Manor Road. Then after a few minutes more, blow me if that car didn't come out again and the motor-bike after it. I thought, I've had enough of this, I thought. They can chase one another round all night long for all I care. I'm going to sleep. So I got up and shut the window. That's all I heard."

Rupert Priggley had thoughtfully been over to the bar for three more drinks and in a moment the fringe of Boggett's moustache had to be wiped.

"Who lives in Manor Lane?" Carolus asked him.

"Well, me to begin with," said Boggett. "You must have seen my house? It used to be the lodge. Then there's Dogman's. Theirs is that house with the wisteria on it. Further on you come to Limpoles' two brothers and a sister and fine old fights you hear coming out of there if one of them's used a spoonful of sugar more than the others. Then there's what they call the Vicarage where those Hopeladys live, though the real Vicarage has been pulled down. Up the other end, opposite side to what the Manor's on, there's an old house been there donkey's years where Scotter the chemist lives, and the joke of it is he's married to my sister. You should have seen their faces when he bought that house. Fact, all the people from this end of the town live in Manor Lane. The only other two are Thriver and Rumble, and they live up Lower Manor Lane, which is a continuation of it across the main road. Here, look at this just come in." Boggett gave Priggley a nudge which nearly sent him off balance. "I couldn't half do with a bit of that. I shall have to see about it. That's what I call something. You wouldn't see me for a week if I got my hands on that lot."

"Bit broad in the beam, isn't she?" said Priggley in the manner of a professional critic.

"Just what you want, my boy, that is. The very thing. What wouldn't I give for it, eh? Exactly my handwriting . . ."

"You were telling me that you worked for Mr. Parador," said Carolus priggishly. The bar would close in ten minutes and he felt Boggett's attention slipping.

"Yes. Yes. I did. Look at those Bristols . . ."

"Were you surprised when you heard about his death?"

"Surprised? I couldn't believe it. I still don't. Not that he did for himself. There's a lot more than meets the eye in this. I daresay if the truth were told I knew him better than anyone and I say he never done it. Never in a million years."

"Then what do you think happened?"

"Ah, now you're asking me. But I think someone who wanted him out of the way did for him somehow we can't know about. Doctors don't know everything, you know. Cor, look at her now. She'll have her skirt round her waist in a minute."

"Did your wife work for Mr. and Mrs. Parador, too?"

"What, Ur? No thank you. Not in the same place where I worked. I told her that. It's bad enough you spying on me at night without the daytime, too, I told her. No, she worked for Rumble. She was there when his wife died two years ago. Well, it suits her. No one behind her all day wanting to know why this wasn't done. It's not like the old days when there wasn't the work. They have to take what help they can get now. And I will say this, Rumble's one to appreciate it. He passed me the other day and remarked on it. 'What I should do without Mrs. Boggett,' he said, 'I don't know.' Nor don't I. A man alone in the house. Look she's having another one. I bet that young fellow with her gets somewhere tonight. I know I would. I'd just about . . ."

"But Mrs. Parador must have some help?"

"Oh yes. She's got a couple of women come up from the new end of town. I don't know why they bother. Their husbands are knocking up the best part of twenty quid a week each on the building. Greedy, I suppose. They're neighbours, see, and like going out together. She only has them for the morning, and once in a while in the afternoon, if they feel like it. But if you want to know all about that you come and see the wife about it. She can tell you, if she likes. She sees all that goes on at Rumble's and she knows these two that work at Parador's. Only thing is she gets tired out before she comes home and doesn't want to talk about anything."

There was a pause, during which levels sank.

" I was looking at that handbag of yours," said Boggett. " The guv'nor had one like that. I noticed it when you came in."

" Did he? Lot of these about now," said Carolus vaguely. Then he turned the subject.

" I believe Miss Thriver used to do some secretarial work for Mr. Parador?"

" Yes, but I couldn't fancy that," said Boggett. " Not that, I couldn't fancy. Too much like those that read things out on the telly. She's as broad as she's long, too. Maybe suit some, but I said the first time I saw her, I said, that's not my line of country. Now if she was anything like that one over there . . ."

" Where did they work?"

" In his study as far as I know. I didn't take much interest to tell you the truth. Must be nearly Time," he added anxiously, with a glance at his empty mug.

Rupert again went to the counter.

" Tell me, Boggett," said Carolus while he was away, and speaking in an earnest voice, " you haven't got any suspicions about Mr. Parador's death, have you? You told me you didn't think it was suicide."

Boggett considered.

" Well, I have and I haven't. He had some business with those Limpoles and they're very funny people. She's not quite all there if you ask me . . ."

" She?"

" That's their sister. The three of them live together. I'd never be surprised to hear they knew more than they said. And I don't trust that vicar. But I wouldn't go so far as to say I had any suspicions. I tell you who might be able to tell you something—that's

Bert Holey. He has the filling-station round the corner. Holey, Holey, Holey, they call him but I don't know why because there's nothing holy about him. He done me out of a lovely little piece of stuff once last summer and I don't forget it. But they all go to him for petrol and I shouldn't be surprised if he was to tell you something if you got him in the right mood."

"Does he come in here?"

"Not very often. Sunday dinner-time he looks in sometimes. His son's home from work then and can look after the pumps. But its my missus *you* should see. If she likes, mind you. You come in tomorrow when she's only been out for an hour in the morning to make the bed and that. Try her round about five. She likes giving anyone a cup of tea. I can't promise you, mind you. But you try."

"Thanks. I will."

Then Boggett gave Carolus a very shrewd look.

"You're from the Insurance, I suppose? I thought as soon as you came in and started asking all those questions that's what you were. Oh well, we all have to do something."

Rupert Priggley showing cool competency in carrying three glasses without spilling any of the contents returned to refresh them just as the barman—Mr. Gray-Somerset remained at the Saloon Bar end—started shouting time.

"There he goes!" said Boggett. "Always the same. I'll bet you it's five minutes short of half past."

Rupert had a question to ask him.

"Did you say Mrs. Parador had a niece staying with her?"

Boggett began to laugh loudly.

"Hark at that! See what I told you? Can't think of anything else, can you? He's a lad, if ever there was one."

"But has she?"

"I told you she had."

"What's she like?"

"He's off again! 'What's she like?' You ought to be thinking about your studies. Wait till you see her. That's all. You wait till you see her."

59

" Any good?"

" I don't know what you mean," said Boggett with mock virtue. " You just wait till you see her."

Priggley said no more, but no one could doubt that he had started waiting.

Chapter Six

IF CAROLUS HAD ONLY THE BEGINNINGS OF A MOST NEBULOUS theory about the death of Felix Parador he was beginning to know a great deal about Brenstead. He had not supposed that by creating a built-to-order background you could change the English way of life, but he had thought to find some difference between the people of Brenstead before its transformation and the people of Brenstead now. He found none except that there were more of them.

Next morning, for instance, a Sunday, he took a walk through the denser streets of houses 'for the workers' and could find nothing new except the buildings. There was little movement on the pavements for the men seemed either to be enjoying their beloved 'Sunday morning lie-in' with tea in bed and the *News of the World* or working in their small oblong gardens. The church bells were audible when there was a pause in the traffic but the scattered mass of people moving in the same direction 'going to church' which he remembered in boyhood was no more. He found it, for all the 'brightness' insisted on by architects, planners and advertisers, a rather dismal place.

At about eleven he went for his car and drove it to the filling-station. He wanted to make the acquaintance of Bert Holey in his place of business so that if he came to The Royal Oak at lunch-time conversation would be easier.

Holey was a tall man, bald on top but with thick clumps of greying hair over his ears. He gazed at the Bentley with a rapt expression.

" Lovely jobs, aren't they?" he ventured.

Carolus was not enough a car man to make one of the expected replies. He couldn't give an off-hand, " Useful, yes," or become enthusiastic about speed and comfort. He never knew what to say about his car and replied rather lamely, " Well, I like it."

" What do you reckon to do to the gallon?"

" I never quite know. It seems to vary."

Bert Holey looked at him with some disapproval, as if to say that Carolus didn't deserve a motor car like that, but brightened up when Carolus asked him to put in all he could.

" You don't happen to be going up to the Oak, do you?" Carolus asked.

" I was just going to get my boy to take over," admitted Holey.

" Like a lift?"

" I'll just change my jacket," said Holey, cutting out any un-necessary verbal flourishes.

He was an interested rather than a talkative passenger but over a drink he began to talk of his customers, which was just what Carolus wanted.

" See, I'm not on the main London road and pretty well half my business is with locals," he said. " I know them all, and they like to be known by name. It makes a lot of difference when you say ' Morning, Mr. Brown ', specially if he's got someone with him. Nearly all of them round here come to me. I see to that. I always know if they've filled up somewhere else."

" Really! How?"

Bert Holey gave a sly grin.

" I'll tell you," he said. " For instance, I don't suppose you know what mileage you've done, do you? But I do." He pulled something like a policeman's notebook out of his pocket and

showed Carolus a figure. " See?" he said triumphantly. " Now
if you was to come in again I shouldn't know whether you'd
filled up or not because I don't know your habits. But with most
of them I do. They're mostly pretty regular."

" You've been doing that for some time?"

" Over a year now. Quite often I pull their legs about it. ' I see
you've been disloyal to the village pump, Mr. So-and-So ', I say.
At first they wondered how I knew then most of them tumbled
to it."

Carolus decided to appear to take Holey into his confidence,
and gave him the Insurance Inspector story. Holey seemed prepared to believe anything of insurance companies and nodded
understandingly.

" What I'd like to know is whether any of them broke their
usual customs on the night Mr. Parador died. Can you give me
any idea about that?"

" Two of them did. I can tell you that straight away without
looking at my book because I saw it for myself. Those Limpoles,
for one. They never use their car except at week-ends. They walk
to the station every morning—for their health they say, but I
know it's just meanness. They're very tight, those two. I saw
them that night, though. 'Bout half-past nine it must have been.
They passed the pumps then looked out and saw me standing
there, and stopped and backed and took a couple of gallons. First
time I'd ever seen them out on a week-day evening."

" Who was the other?"

" Hopelady the vicar, in that old Triumph of his. He didn't call
here but I saw him go by."

" Alone?"

" Yes. And next morning I reckoned he'd been about twenty
miles by his tank and mileage."

" What about Mr. Parador's car? Did you get a chance to see
that?"

" Only after the police had brought it in. I thought they might
have been running about in it, but no, it was just right to have
been out to the Great Ring and back again. Who else do you
want to know about?"

" Mr. Thriver."

" Couldn't have done more than a mile or two. The doctor you can't tell with because he's got no regular habits."

" What about Rumble?"

" He doesn't come to me any more. Must be about a month ago now we had words. I'm a man who never quarrels if he can help it, but he seemed to pick on me all about nothing. So I can't tell you."

" You've been very helpful," said Carolus. " You see, whatever else this affair is, it's local. So I'm naturally interested in the movements of people here."

" I can quite see that," conceded Bert Holey. " You're welcome to anything I might be able to tell you from what I've got in the old notebook."

Carolus saw that from the other side of the room Boggett was making violent signs to him and made his way across.

" Only, me and Bert Holey are Not Speaking," was his greeting to Carolus. " Not since that dirty trick he done me over that one I told you about."

" You wanted to tell me something?"

" Yes. It's the missus. I think it will be All Right."

" What will?"

" You coming round this afternoon. I told her there was a gentleman popping in."

" What did she say?"

" Well, you know what she is. Began sighing and moaning and saying she supposed she'd have to give you a cup of tea and have all the washing-up to do after."

" It doesn't sound very hopeful."

" You don't know her," Boggett contradicted himself. " That's a good sign when she talks like that. If she'd said nothing I shouldn't have liked the look of things at all. But when she has her grouse like that it may turn out for the best. You can only try."

" Exactly."

" And mind you, she *can* tell you things. If once she starts, that is."

But when Carolus reached Boggett's cottage at five o'clock that afternoon, Boggett, who opened the door, seemed far less hopeful.

"I'm afraid it won't be much good," he whispered. "She's had a nap this afternoon and woke up in a nasty mood. She hasn't *said* much but I can tell. Still, you better come in."

Carolus found a large woman with a fat, dough-like face sitting in an arm-chair by the fire. Boggett's introduction was oblique.

"Here he is," he said to his wife. "I told him you could tell him more than what I could."

"Afternoon," said Mrs. Boggett in a wheezy voice, looking at Carolus without enthusiasm.

"He's trying to find out all about Mr. Parador's death for the insurance company," Boggett went on encouragingly.

Mrs. Boggett addressed her husband.

"I suppose you want a cup of tea," she said disapprovingly.

"The gentleman would . . ."

"That means I shall have to go and put the kettle on," sighed Mrs. Boggett, and began to ease her bulk from her chair. "You always want something," she added, rising slowly to her feet, her stertorous breathing audible across the room. "Never give me five minutes to myself." She stumped towards the door.

Boggett seemed delighted.

"She's coming round," he said. "I told you she would."

In a few minutes Mrs. Boggett returned carrying a huge tray. She must have spent some time earlier in preparing this, cutting bread and butter, perhaps getting out her best china. It was a bountiful tea and there was home-made jam.

"I don't know," she sighed. "It seems only a few minutes since you had your dinner. Talk about the day of rest. Go on—hand the gentleman the bread and butter while I'm pouring out. How many spoons of sugar?" she asked Carolus. "I know *he* likes three. There you are, then."

"Tell him what you've heard," said Boggett impatiently.

His wife ignored this.

"I'm afraid there's not much to offer you," she told Carolus, but it was of the tea she was speaking, not information. "Boggett thinks I've got all day to spend looking after things. He doesn't know what work is."

Carolus decided to try his luck.

"Mrs. Boggett, you work for Mr. Rumble, I believe?"

"You must ask my husband about that," said Mrs. Boggett touchily. "He knows about everything, he does. He'll tell you."

"Oh, come on. Tell the man what you know," challenged Boggett.

"Ready for some more tea? That's right. It's no good asking me about anything like that. Not but what I don't notice things."

"You know the two that work where I do at Parador's, don't you?" said Boggett provokingly.

"I'm not saying I do and I'm not saying I don't." Then suddenly to Carolus, "What is it you want to know?"

"He wants to know anything you can tell him," put in Boggett tactlessly.

This seemed to scotch Mrs. Boggett's intention to confide.

"Tell him? You know very well I haven't the time for a lot of gossip. I've got too much to do. It's as much as I can do to get round to my work every day let alone join in a lot of chit-chat."

"How do you get to work every day?" asked Carolus politely, trying to approach through general channels.

"I've got a scooter," said Mrs. Boggett surprisingly. "But it takes it out of you. I have to do every blessed thing at Mr. Rumble's, too. He can't do anything in the house and since his wife died he has no one to turn to. If it wasn't for me I don't know where he'd be."

"What about his breakfast in the morning?"

"He can make himself a cup of tea. That much he learned in the army, I suppose. But I have to leave his Evening Meal all ready for him. *Then* he doesn't eat half of it. I get him some nice cold ham or something like that and when I come in the morning I find he's only eaten . . ."

"He doesn't want to hear about what Rumble eats," said Boggett. "Tell him about Scotter and the parcel."

"I'll tell him what I think fit and he can take it or leave it," said Mrs. Boggett. "What I was going to say was the only time

66

I've known him eat all I left out was the night Mr. Parador was done for."

"Why do you say ' done for ', Mrs. Boggett?"

"So he was. I don't believe all that about sleeping pills. Someone did for him. They've got so many ways now . . . I've seen it on the telly. Injections and that. Things no one knows anything about and leave no trace. All they've got to do is to knock them unconscious then do it with gas from the exhaust of his car. No one's safe, really. Not with a man like Scotter there to supply everything you need."

"She doesn't like Scotter," explained Boggett.

"Nasty sneaking kind of man, I've always said. And what he thinks of himself: supposed to be all on the side of Labour and ashamed of his own brother-in-law. He married Boggett's sister— and a nicer woman you couldn't meet—when he was quite a young man, before he knew he was going to get where he is. You should see him if we happen to meet in the street anywhere. You know what I heard from Mrs. Byles and Mrs. Pocock . . ."

"Never mind about Mrs. Byles and Mrs. Pocock. Tell him about the parcel."

"If you don't keep quiet I shan't tell him anything at all. So now then. This Mrs. Byles and Mrs. Pocock are the two ladies that help Mrs. Parador. You should see them together! There's Mrs. Byles as tall as a telegraph post and Mrs. Pocock a funny little thing no bigger than her own daughter. I see them sometimes at the kayfe in the afternoon. It was them told me about this parcel Scotter brought for Mr. Parador and give to him himself. Now what's Scotter doing bringing parcels, that's what I should like to know. He's too high and mighty to talk to anyone but he delivers something from his shop. Doesn't make sense."

"What did I tell you?" Boggett asked Carolus proudly. "I told you she'd have something to tell if she got going."

"This Mrs. Byles and Mrs. Pocock," went on Mrs. Boggett. "Told me a lot of things about what's supposed to have gone on before Mr. Parador was done for. I let them talk. It was only when they began about where I work that I turned on them because that's as good as saying something to me."

"You mean about Mr. Rumble?"

"That's what they said it was, but it was meant for me. I know that very well. Saying there was something between him and Mrs. Parador and had been for a long time. I turned on them pretty quick when they said that. 'You be careful what you're saying', I told them. So then they got on to the vicar."

"Really?"

"Yes. It seems there was words once between him and Mr. Parador. This Mr. Hopelady's a man who likes a joke and tried it on with Mr. Parador. You should have heard him shout, Mrs. Byles and Mrs. Pocock said. You could hear it all over the house. 'Get out, you snivelling bible-thumper!' Mr. Parador shouted, so Mrs. Byles and Mrs. Pocock said, and they never expected to see him come to the house again. But he was up there on the very afternoon of the day Mr. Parador was murdered. Trying to get a subscription for something from Mrs. Parador. At least that's what it sounded like to Mrs. Byles and Mrs. Pocock because they heard her say she was sorry she had so many calls on her, and they said Mr. Hopelady came away with a face as long as a poker."

There was no need for Carolus to say encouraging words or for Boggett to challenge. Mrs. Boggett had Got Going.

"Then those Limpoles," she said. "The three of them's so mean they half-starve themselves rather than buy proper food. *She* does all the work. The elder brother Charles never goes out if he can help it. The younger one, Edward, would be just the same if it wasn't for his garden. He loves that, I must say. I saw him the other day as I happened to be passing the house and there he was talking to Mrs. Parador who was taking her dog out for a walk and must have gone in to look at something. They were both of them stooping down but what they were staring at I *don't* know. The other brother and the sister were nowhere in sight otherwise they'd have had something to say. She's not quite all there if the truth were known."

"Who? Miss Limpole?"

"That's it. Going off for walks at all hours of the day and night. Coming in when it's nearly getting light. Boggett will tell you about that. He's out half the night, very often. All I know is, she's Been Seen. You don't know what to think, do you?"

"Yes," said Carolus disconcertingly.

"Well, I'm sure I don't. You know Mr. Parador gave Boggett the sack once, don't you?"

"There's no need to bring that up again," said Boggett.

"Didn't he tell you?"

"It was only because of the lawn."

"That's what Mr. Parador said it was but you know very well it was Something Else."

"It was Ur done it," said Boggett, referring once again, apparently to that ancient city of the Chaldees.

"No it wasn't anything of the sort. You know very well why it was. Why should Mrs. Parador have wanted to get rid of you, anyway?"

"I knew too much for her liking."

Mrs. Boggett wheezed angrily.

"*You* knew too much. You don't know your arse from your elbow if the truth were told." She turned to Carolus. "It was him shooting his mouth off at the Oak, if you want to know. *And* getting half-sozzled at dinner-time that day and going to mow the lawn all in zig-zags so that when Mr. Parador came home he thought he'd been having a game of snakes and ladders. That's what it was and he can't say different."

Boggett winked vigorously to Carolus.

"I don't know what else you want to know," reflected Mrs. Boggett. "I could always ask Mrs. Byles and Mrs. Pocock anything you wanted. They're quite obliging when it comes to it. At least Mrs. Byles is, I don't know about Mrs. Pocock so much. They're about the only two go out to work any more. Thrivers do their own, though I don't know how they manage, and the sister works for those two Limpoles. As for the vicar, he wouldn't get anyone even if he could afford it, not with all those children. Little feens they are, too."

"How, little fiends?"

"So they are. There was two of them grinning all over their faces at me the other morning when I was trying to start my scooter. 'I'll give you good as a circus', I told them. It was a good thing their father came along just then and apologised else I might have done them an injury."

Carolus looked at his watch.

"I have to go to a cocktail party at Mrs. Dogman's," he said.

"That'll be nice," said Mrs. Boggett. "I wouldn't go not if they was to go down on their bended knees and asked me. Lot of gossip-mongering la-di-dah women talking about those that aren't there. I know—I heard last time What Was Said. You won't find me taking people's reputation away like that behind their backs. She'll be half-drunk as likely as not. It wouldn't be the first time. As for *him*, I don't know what to say. He's No Good, if you ask me. They'll all be there though, and some you don't know about. Thrivers, Mrs. Parador, Dr. Sporlott. All of them."

"What about the Limpoles?"

"They never Touch Anything but I shouldn't be surprised because there's bound to be something to eat which they won't have to pay for. Nor wouldn't I be surprised if Scotter's there, though his wife wouldn't go, I do know that. Then there's the vicar . . ."

"Surely not, on Sunday evening?"

"Oh yes, after Church, he will. He'd never miss anything. And his wife. They lock the children up in the attic when they go out . . ."

"Really, Mrs. Boggett, are you sure of that?"

"That's what I've Been Told, anyway."

Carolus rose to say good-bye and thank his hostess.

"That's all right," said Mrs. Boggett. "So long as you don't expect me to talk a lot of gossip I don't mind telling you what I happen to know. I'll have a word with Mrs. Byles and Mrs. Pocock when I see them. If anything turns up I daresay Boggett will know where to find you."

Carolus found Rupert Priggley sitting in the car.

"I thought I might as well just have a glance at the niece," he explained casually.

They set off for the Dogmans' home.

Chapter Seven

THE DOGMANS' HOUSE WAS NOT LARGE, BUT HAVING A MODERN
Georgian type front and standing a little way back from the road
it looked very much a ' gentleman's residence '. Carolus drove in.

He rang the bell, and a woman in a noisy frock, wearing a gay
auburn wig came to the door.

" Oh darling, you should have walked straight in. I don't know
who you are but somebody must have asked you."

" Yes, you did," said Carolus, assuming this to be Chatty Dogman. " You phoned me at lunch-time today. My name's Deene.
This is Rupert Priggley."

" Did I, darling? Yes, the name does sound somehow familiar.
Do come in and have a drink. You'll find one over there. Talk to
somebody, won't you? There aren't enough men, but then there
never are, are there?"

She disappeared among her guests.

Carolus found himself in a long room, fairly crowded. He
located the drinks which were on a brand new refectory table,
presided over by a man in a check suit.

" Hullo, did the wife send you over for a drink? That's right.

Let me pour it for you. I suppose you're a friend of hers. I'm afraid we haven't met, or have we? I'm Willy James Dogman."

Carolus explained how he came to be there but Dogman only paid enough attention to be polite.

" I'm staying at The Royal Oak," finished Carolus lamely.

" The Royal Oak? That's a ghastly pub. What are you staying there for?"

A difficult question.

" Oh, just for a night or two," said Carolus apologetically.

" Can't stand that type who keeps it. Never have liked liars," said Dogman.

They were interrupted by Chatty.

" Darling, give me two nice stiff gin and tonics, will you? Your friend Scotter's dying of thirst."

" So he wants two, does he?" said Dogman laughing noisily.

" Come along, darling. A little more gin—that's right. Christ, there's Elspeth arriving with her niece."

Carolus turned to see a handsome woman bearing down on them. Elspeth Parador was very nearly a beauty and full of charm. As soon as Carolus was introduced she drew him away.

" I know all about you," she said. " Maggie phoned me. We all call my brother-in-law Maggie. He loathes it."

" I'm not surprised. I'm glad he remembered to phone you."

" Yes, and I'm glad you've come. It would be wonderful if you could prove my old Felix didn't commit suicide. I thought the inquest was a farce."

Carolus noticed that Rupert and Elspeth's niece, a rather vacantly pretty girl of eighteen were already in conversation.

" You don't think I'm a heartless brute to come to a party so soon, do you? I adored Felix but honestly, he wouldn't want me to go on weeping for ever."

" Not at all," said Carolus. " I quite understand that you want to get out."

" Thank you," said Elspeth warmly. " I'm sure we're going to get on. When can we meet and really have a talk? I don't think I've a lot to tell you but I'll try."

" Tomorrow?" suggested Carolus.

"Yes. Come and have a cup of tea or something. About four?"

"I'd love to."

"You must meet everyone here. Chatty will never remember to introduce you. You know the Thrivers?"

"Yes, Magnus rang them too."

"Then I give you your choice. Both a bit quaint. Over by the mantelpiece is Edward Limpole and his sister. And quite alone in front of that bookcase is our local chemist, Mr. Scotter. You've probably heard of both."

"I have. May I try the Limpoles first?"

"Come on, then. We can leave the children here."

Edward Limpole did not look quite the old-fashioned puritan of his reputation. He was thin and narrow and wore rimless glasses. He looked serious, even rather worried, but there was something kind and friendly in his smile and Carolus wondered whether it was quite natural. For his sister the only adjective was gaunt.

"Edward. Nora. I want you to meet Mr. Deene."

Edward Limpole tried to give a greeting but seemed confused. His sister blinked with some hostility.

Carolus could be socially cruel and decided to let the brother or sister break the silence. At last a question came—from Edward.

"Are you interested in gardening, Mr. Deene?"

"I'm no expert."

Nora Limpole spoke without ceasing to stare at the top of the far wall.

"My brother thinks of nothing else." She had a peculiar voice, like a horse quietly neighing.

"And you?" asked Carolus politely.

"It bores me stiff."

"My sister doesn't really mean that."

"Oh, yes I do. It was the garden I quarrelled with Felix over."

Sweat was on Edward Limpole's forehead and he tried to interrupt, but Carolus seemed interested. "Really?" he said encouragingly.

73

"Yes. I told him he ought to be ashamed of himself spending thousands on an ornamental patch of ground when children are dying of starvation."

"I don't suppose he liked that?" said Carolus fatuously.

"He deserved it. He could start nearer home if he didn't want to support Oxfam. I don't think the Hopelady children get enough to eat."

"Nora," said her brother in open consternation. "You really mustn't say such things. Mr. and Mrs. Hopelady will be here presently."

"I say what I believe to be true."

"My sister is a qualified nurse," said Edward helplessly, as though that explained everything.

"I've seen suffering, Mr. Deene."

"Most of us have, in one form or another."

"I sometimes wonder if my brothers have. They're so complacent."

Carolus was relieved to see Chatty Dogman coming across.

"I'd like to see your garden if I may," he said to Edward before she reached them.

Edward brightened up.

"Please do. It's not very much but I've got some interesting things. I'm going to be at home all next week so come when you like."

Nora was looking into the distance again.

"Darlings," said Chatty. "You've all got empty glasses. What's yours, Edward? Scotch? No, of course you don't. All right, lemonade. Nora? The same? *You'll* have a drink, won't you, darling? I forget your name. Do come across and get it. Willy James will be incapable of pouring out in a minute. Wait, I could do with another myself."

Carolus followed her to the refectory table.

"Darling, this poor man's dying of thirst. And just a teeny one for me."

"You'll be tight," said Willy James bluntly.

"I like that, coming from you."

Elspeth joined them.

74

"How did you get on?" she asked Carolus with a smile.

"Oh, very well. She told me about her quarrel with your late husband."

Elspeth's smile disappeared and she looked suddenly unhappy.

"I know it's silly," she said, "but I'm still not used to hearing old Felix called my late husband. Yes, they did have a row. Felix *could* be a little quarrelsome, you know, but I think this was her fault. She's really a bit eccentric. Now you deserve to meet someone nice, so I shan't introduce Scotter yet. He's nice, I suppose, but so prickly. Jimmie! Come here and meet Mr. Deene. He's been suffering under the Limpole yoke. This is Jimmy Rumble. He's been a pet to me since it happened, though we scarcely knew each other before."

Carolus faced a smallish man with an open face and a clipped, slightly greying moustache, very much what used to be called a gentleman, meaning that he had been at a good school and perhaps in a good regiment.

When they were a little apart from the rest, Rumble said, "Elspeth tells me you're going to get at the truth about Felix's death."

"Yes. If I can."

"I quite agree it probably wasn't suicide. The only thing that worries me is . . . suppose it turns out to be anything else . . ."

"Murder, you mean?"

"Yes, I suppose so. Don't you think that might be even worse for Elspeth? Frankly, she's my only interest in the case. I'd almost rather see a murderer get away with it than have her upset again."

"I see what you mean. But is the truth even worse than doubt?"

"It's a tough question. I never got on too well with Felix. It's only since this happened I've been seeing much of Elspeth. I don't think he approved of me."

"Why not?"

"Not for any particular reason, perhaps. He wasn't altogether an easy man to get on with. Some years ago I bought a travel agency, chiefly to give me something to do, really. He pretty well called me a fool to throw my money away. ' Foreign travel's a passing craze ', he said. But that's all forgotten now."

" Didn't you point out that it was a passing craze which has gone on ever since man could stand upright?"

" He wasn't a man you could argue with."

Somehow the two of them were drawn into a group in which were Enid and Patsy Thriver. He saw that Patsy was going to speak as though they shared a secret and was pleased to find himself being introduced to a man and wife he had not seen before and, as it happened, never saw again.

At that moment there was sudden darkness. There were no screams, though the buzz of conversation rose in pitch and grew louder.

Chatty's voice could be heard above the rest, sounding a little hysterical.

" God, Willy James! Can't you do something? Put a new fuse in! I don't know where I put my drink."

Patsy spoke in a low voice to Carolus.

" One always finds there has been a murder when the lights come on," she said.

But there had not been a murder. It was only the manner in which the Reverend George Hopelady announced himself. He knew the main switch was in the hall and he was having one of his jokes.

" Good evening! Good evening to you all!" he cried entering joyfully, his flushed, bony little wife following him into the room.

There was some relief and a little laughter from his supporters, but one could not say that the vicar had had a wild success. Rupert Priggley who with Elspeth's niece had been helping Chatty by carrying a huge tray of food into the room had been caught in mid passage unable to set down the tray. He was frankly furious.

" I wouldn't have minded so much if I'd had my hands free," he confided in Carolus later.

Mr. Hopelady had a neck which grew like a thin pink stalk out of his clerical collar. His face was all teeth and cheek-bones, the chin receding woefully. Carolus watched him without affection as he made his round of the guests, greeting everyone—not effusively but as though certain of his own popularity.

"He's a crashing bore," said Patsy. "And of course means well. He'll have some jolly pleasantry for you when he gets round to us."

Hearing this, Rupert Priggley seemed about to make for the door but Carolus restrained him because Elspeth's niece, unfortunately known as Bunty, was already half-way upstairs.

"You can't do that," Carolus said.

At that moment Mr. Hopelady reached them and unfortunately chose Rupert as his victim, stopping to speak in his ear.

"Excuse me, old chap, but your zip's open," he said.

Rupert's reaction was admirably swift.

"So's your mouth," he said truthfully, and picking up a block of ice-cream from the table beside him he rammed it between Mr. Hopelady's jaws, already wide in anticipation of laughter.

There was a scream from Mrs. Hopelady, but her husband's splutterings and chokings alarmed her and she led him from the room.

"Darling," said Chatty to Rupert, "that was rather beastly of you. Funny, I suppose, but not very polite. However, have a drink, darling."

When Mr. Hopelady returned he came up to Carolus as the responsible adult.

"I did not think that was very funny," he said severely.

"Not a bit funny," echoed his wife. "The suit will have to go to the cleaners."

"No, it was not respectful," agreed Carolus. "But I'm afraid there was a certain amount of provocation."

"Provocation? A harmless little leg-pull like that? Has your son no sense of humour?"

"Priggley is *not* my son," said Carolus.

"Well, whatever he is. That's what's lacking in the modern generation of youngsters. They can't take a joke against themselves."

"It's a common failing," said Carolus mildly.

"If you mean George," said Mrs. Hopelady furiously, "he's

the *first* to laugh when someone pulls his leg. But that wasn't a joke. It might have been dangerous."

The vicar seemed to realise that it was time to beam magnanimously. " Anyway, no harm done," he said. " We mustn't get heated over ice-cream."

" Priggley, you owe Mr. Hopelady an apology," said Carolus.

" I'm sorry, sir," said Priggley rather too readily. " But don't ever, *ever* play practical jokes on me again. Can I get you a drink?"

Mr. Hopelady smiled.

" A rather mixed form of apology," he said. " But yes, I should like something warming. A little Scotch perhaps?"

" Ice?" asked Priggley, but there was no reply.

" I wanted to have a talk with you if you can spare the time," Carolus told the vicar. " Could I call on you, perhaps?"

" Delighted. Please do. Tomorrow if you wish. I shall be at home all day." Then rather anxiously, " Anything urgent?"

" Don't bring that detestable boy with you," said Mrs. Hopelady.

Carolus, having arranged to call at the vicarage in the morning, crossed the room to where Mr. Scotter, a tall unsmiling man in his forties, stood alone.

" May I introduce myself?" he said, and did so.

" I've been watching that little incident," said Scotter. " It was time someone did something like that. I don't like larks."

" I'm not mad on them myself."

" I'm not a believer in conventional religion, but when a man receives a salary as a minister of a church he should behave like one," continued Mr. Scotter severely. " I expect you're wondering what a man like me is doing in a place like this. I feel that the modern man should be able to move up and down the scale."

" And which is this? Up? Or down?" asked Carolus wondering when Mr. Scotter would make a remark that did not start with ' I '.

" I come from the Masses, myself," continued Mr. Scotter, " but I don't feel out of place in any society. I told the late Mr. Parador . . ."

" How did you get on with him?"

" I respected his position and he respected mine."

" He was a customer of yours?"

" I had the pleasure of supplying him, yes. I found him somewhat opinionated, of course. I don't think he agreed with me politically speaking, but I was pleased that he invited me to his house on several occasions."

Carolus did not think this the time or the place to ask any more questions and in any case was interrupted by the last and most surprising event of that disturbed occasion. His back was to the door, but he saw Mr. Scotter stiffen. His eyes opened wide and he so far forgot himself, quite literally, that he asked a question.

" Who's this?"

Carolus turned and saw in the doorway a woman in her thirties. She looked either doped or drunk and she was wearing a fur coat and a hat. It seemed that she was a stranger for a silence fell over the room and everyone watched the newcomer.

" Is she here?" she asked in a loud, dramatic voice. " I want to speak to Elspeth Parador."

Elspeth stood up. It was like an old-fashioned play.

" Henrietta!" she said. " Whatever's the matter?"

" As if you didn't know!"

Elspeth remained calm and looked somewhat disgusted.

" Are you drunk?" she asked the woman. They did not approach one another but talked across several people as though unaware of an audience.

" Yes. I am rather. But I was determined to see you. *You drove him to it.*"

" What on earth are you talking about?"

" I'm talking about Felix. I loved him just as much as you. You drove him to it, I said, and I meant it."

" I think you had better go away," said Elspeth with admirable calm.

" Yes, you can't come here like this, whoever you are," said Willy James Dogman, moving towards her.

Henrietta Ballard ignored him, and addressed Elspeth again.

79

"Don't pretend you don't know. You introduced us yourself. Where do you think he used to go at night? You made his life hell."

"Did he tell you that?" asked Elspeth.

"No. He believed in you. I supposed you told him he had to leave me?"

Elspeth lost her calm.

"I did not know . . . I hadn't heard of you for years . . ." she said rather brokenly.

"Then you stopped him giving me what he promised. He's left me without a sou and it's all your doing!"

Willy James had reached her now, supported by James Rumble.

"You must go," he said. "You can't come to my house and shout like that."

"I'll go," said Henrietta Ballard. "I've said what I want."

She turned towards the door.

"But she'll hear more from me. Or my s'licitors."

It looked as though she was going to stumble through the door but she made it.

Carolus joined the group round Elspeth. She was being given a brandy and much sympathy.

"It's true," she said tearfully. "I did introduce them . . . but I'd no idea. I don't believe it of Felix."

"She was drunk," said Rumble.

"I know . . . but she *said* those things." Elspeth had been so calm during the attack that the reaction, now that it came, was violent. "I won't have her saying I drove him to it . . . my dear old Felix. It's wicked. And he *didn't* leave her without a sou. She was always deceitful, even when I first knew her. I don't believe Felix used to go . . . oh it's too beastly. Chatty, dear, I'm sorry your party's been upset . . ."

"Don't worry about that, darling," said Chatty. "What you want is another little drink. Willy James, do give Elspeth a drink, darling. She just needs a drink."

"No, dear. I want to go home. I'm . . . it was . . . *please* let me go home."

Chapter Eight

BUT THAT WAS NOT QUITE THE END OF THE PARTY. CHATTY DOG-
man was making vigorous gesticulations to Rupert Priggley and
Bunty and they appeared with another tray of food towards
which Mr. Hopelady and his wife edged their way. Rumble had
taken Elspeth home, but the Thrivers remained and Carolus was
with them.

"Seen any more faces at the window?" he asked Patsy.

"No. Wasn't I absurd? I still jump every time I hear a motor-
bike."

"Is that often?"

"Not up our road. But there are plenty on the main road. One
woke me up the other night, just under my window, I thought
it was."

Thriver called Carolus aside.

"I suppose that's the new beneficiary," he said.

"Yes, if the will turns up."

"Dreadful young woman."

"I don't think she was drunk," said Carolus. "I was watching
her carefully. It may have been marijuana."

" Whatever it was she must have had some object in coming here and making a scene. Elspeth was wonderful, I thought. Terrible thing for her. She's a very plucky woman. Enid, dear, we ought to be going."

" Yes, Graham. I'm trying to think where I put my—ah, there they are. Patsy, your father says we must go. It's not far to walk."

" Mumsie, we've got the car."

They said good night to Chatty who said she was awfully sorry without specifying the cause. Mr. Scotter followed them out. Carolus gave him enough time to be out of the way then said his good nights and thanks. Rupert Priggley, after reminding Bunty of their date tomorrow, followed.

" I'm going to take her primrosing tomorrow," he told Carolus. " In Langley Wood."

" You? Primrosing?"

" Why not? I *like* primrosing. Lovely little spring flowers. The trouble with you, sir, is that you have no romance in you."

Next morning at breakfast Rupert Priggley had the politeness to ask Carolus what he intended to do.

" Just odd bits and pieces."

" Then I know you're getting warm. I know those odd bits and pieces of yours. They always lead to the heart of the matter. Who are you going to see?"

" The vicar, perhaps. Edward Limpole's garden. That sort of thing. Loose ends, you might say."

" I might, but I know better. What I want to know is—when is something going to happen?"

" I don't know what you mean," said Carolus. " We haven't been here three days and already you've had a man run down by a car, a face peering in at the window of a solicitor's house, a vicar with an ice-cream rammed down his throat and a woman gate-crashing a party to tell another woman she was being kept by her husband, or something like it. What more do you want?"

" Murder," said Priggley, " or what are we wasting our time for?"

" Oh go primrosing," said Carolus.

The vicarage was a modest villa in Manor Lane and its garden looked like a school playground. The door was opened by a fat boy of twelve who was in such a hurry to join some activity out of sight that he interrupted Carolus before he had finished asking for his father and pointed to a door saying, "He's in there." Then raised his voice to shout, "COMING!"

"I'm afraid they've no manners," said Mr. Hopelady, appearing in the doorway. "Do come in. Take a pew. Have a cigar?"

There was only one in the box and something told Carolus it would explode as soon as it was lit.

"You don't mind if I smoke my own? I'm used to them."

The vicar was downcast but let it pass.

"Now what can I do for you?" he asked.

Carolus gave him the insurance company bit at some length then appealed for his help in clearing up one or two little scraps of information.

"Of course. Anything I can tell you," said Mr. Hopelady, who seemed to be having a lot of trouble with his pipe.

"First about the night on which Felix Parador was . . . died."

"Ye . . . e . . . e . . . s?" said the vicar on two notes, his eyes still on the bowl of his pipe.

"Did you have occasion to go out that night?"

"Out? Certainly not. I never go out at night."

"By 'night', I mean in the late evening."

"Certainly not after ten. Never."

They were interrupted by the crew of a space ship which had apparently earthed in the garden. But the vicar was equal to it.

"No! No! I told you!" His voice had an edge to it such as Carolus had only heard when he had complained of Priggley yesterday. "I can't be an inhabitant of Mars this morning. I'm far too busy."

"We're going to put his car into orbit then," said an astronaut grimly.

"You'll do nothing of the sort," said the vicar. He went to the door and called his wife, who appeared in a moment but with wet hands. "Willa, I wish you'd not let them play these interstellar games. I'm busy this morning."

Willa's flush deepened.

"You taught them, dear. They've left Elizabeth tied up by the leg in the back garden. She's got to be twenty minutes in space, they say, and the poor child's crying her eyes out."

"I only taught them to keep them out of the house. Matthew! Luke! Ann! What shall I tell them to do?" asked the vicar desperately.

"Go primrosing," suggested Carolus. "I'll give them sixpence a bunch for what they gather in Langley Wood."

There was a united screech and the space ship was abandoned.

"Now where were we?" asked the vicar.

"You were just saying that you were not out after ten o'clock on the night Felix Parador died," Carolus reminded him.

"I said I was never—but wait a minute. There was one night when I was called out to see old Mrs. Grantham."

"Yes?" said Carolus watching him intently.

"Dying, poor soul. Her sister telephoned for me. Twice, in fact. Could it be? Yes, I believe it *was* the night Parador died."

"You went, of course?"

"Indeed yes. Although she lived five miles out. I was there for an hour the first time and no sooner had I got home than she phoned again. It must have been well past midnight when I finally got to bed."

"Did Mrs. Grantham recover?"

"I fear not. She died two days later. I buried her."

"She lived alone with her sister?"

"She lived quite alone for many years. Her sister had come to nurse her."

"Where is the sister now?"

"Went back to America, I understand. She knew no one here. Except, of course, Dr. Sporlott. A splendid fellow, that."

"I wonder if you noticed anything at all unusual when you were out that night, Mr. Hopelady?"

"Dear me! Is it as serious as that? Almost an interrogation, one might say. No, I observed nothing."

"You were not on speaking terms with Parador, I believe?"

"You heard last night. A ridiculous little dispute. I chanced to have a very lifelike representation of a poisonous snake in my pocket one day when I went to see him. Just a little joke of mine, but unfortunately very lifelike. I did not know that Parador had an absolute terror of snakes of all kinds. His experiences in the East, I daresay. He saw it and really behaved like a lunatic. I tried to explain and picked the thing up, but this made it worse. When he realised the truth he ordered me out of the house. He had no sense of humour, you know."

" I see. But he was the godfather of one of your children?"

" Yes. Mark. No, Matthew."

" One other question which will seem to you quite idiotic . . ."

" I'm bound to admit I don't quite see where this is leading. But go on, my dear fellow. I'm quite willing to answer if it is helpful."

" I think you called on Mrs. Parador that afternoon."

" Which afternoon?"

" Of the same day. The day you went to Mrs. Grantham's sick-bed. The day of Parador's death."

" Did I? I may have."

Willa Hopelady entered with a tray on which were two cups of pale beige coffee with some arrowroot biscuits. Carolus feared she might join them, but she went out closing the door. Mr. Hopelady had had time to remember.

" Yes!" he cried. " You're quite right. It was that afternoon. I called on our dear Elspeth."

" Would you mind telling me if you had any particular reason?"

Carolus thought there was something a little sly on the vicar's usually innocent face. He seemed to be wondering how much Carolus knew.

" Yes," he said thoughtfully. " I had something in mind. I liked calling on Elspeth. We all do. She's a great favourite in the parish. But I hoped to persuade her to act as peacemaker between me and her husband. It was so ridiculous to keep up a quarrel over nothing. I thought she would be as glad as I to put an end to it."

" Did she agree?"

"Oh yes. She said he wouldn't be coming down that evening but she would talk to him when she had a chance. Unfortunately, as you know, she never had a chance."

"What did she mean when she said he had so many calls on him?"

"Really! You *are* well-informed. I don't remember her saying that but it may have referred to something else. It is one of my unfortunate duties to ask for subscriptions for our various local charities. I may have just mentioned some deserving cause."

"I see. I'm most grateful to you, Mr. Hopelady . . ."

"You haven't drunk your coffee! My wife won't forgive me if you spurn our simple hospitality."

Carolus made an effort.

"I have to see Limpole," he explained.

"The younger? Ah, yes. He's at home this week. I hope your efforts are successful. And thanks for your ingenuity in thinking of primrosing. I'm afraid you may have more than you bargained for. It depends on the size of the bunches, of course."

"It's raining!" said Carolus as the vicar began to open the front door, then realised that a watering can was spraying water from an upstairs window.

"Ha! ha!" Mr. Hopelady's laugh followed Carolus out to his car. "Ha! ha!" he shouted at Carolus's wet shoulders and head. Even as Carolus took his seat he could still hear it, a mite hysterical, mocking, moronic, ha, ha, ha.

It was not many yards to the Limpoles' house and from its gate he could see Edward far down the garden. He passed the front door and went across a lawn to find Edward gazing with satisfaction on a deep cavity he seemed to have made.

"Oh, good morning, Mr. Deene. You gave me quite a start. I had just finished digging."

"It looks like a grave," said Carolus truthfully.

"It's a compost dump," said Edward seriously. "I wanted a large one. I've taken this week off from business to do several little jobs in the garden."

"I hope your brother won't mind my coming straight down here?"

" My brother has gone to London as usual and my sister is out."

" So your place will be empty in that railway carriage this morning," reflected Carolus.

" We don't seem to travel together so regularly since poor Parador Passed On," said Edward. " None of us can ever forget our somewhat eerie experience. That young man who got in . . ."

" Young?"

" He gave me that impression."

" Please go on."

" It was not so much what he said. Anyone might have said that—meaning that the train was about to start and the other passenger would not be in time. It was the way he said it and the way he acted. It makes me uncomfortable when I think of it. I try to assure myself that it had no significance, but I cannot forget it."

Carolus seemed to be absorbed by the shape of the cavity in front of them, but he looked up to see Edward staring at the brief-case.

" That looks like the one Parador used to carry," said Edward.

Carolus smiled.

" Doesn't it?" he said.

Edward recovered himself.

" I have only one thing I want to show you," said Edward. " *Unctualia petualis.* They have it at Kew I believe, but otherwise this is unique in the British Isles. It's Tibetan by origin. Let's go across to the greenhouse."

Carolus, who had suffered from gardeners before, followed obediently. But in the greenhouse after a brief look round, his attention became riveted—not on *unctualia petualis,* an insignificant blue flower with spotted foliage—but on a small cupboard. The door had a lock to it but had been carelessly left open by Edward, for the keys were in it. On the shelf of the cupboard was a tube of Opilactic.

" Oh *that,*" said Edward, following the direction of Carolus's stare. " I got that for my poor sister. My brother disapproves strongly of any kind of sleeping tablet so I keep it out here. I daresay you noticed that my sister is somewhat highly-strung."

Carolus said nothing, and Edward talked on.

" We're both very worried about her, Mr. Deene. She behaves in a most eccentric way sometimes. Without any explanation or warning to us she goes for long walks, often at night."

" Yes. That must be disconcerting."

" It happened on the very night of Parador's death. When we returned from London she was not here. We waited until past nine o'clock then decided that we should go and look for her. Fortunately she usually keeps to the roads so there was a fair chance of finding her.

Carolus listened, apparently fascinated. But Edward broke off for a moment.

" I'm afraid I cannot offer you anything," he said. " We are all strict teetotallers. But if you would care to come into the house we can at least be comfortable."

Seated in an arm-chair Edward continued.

" My brother does not like using the car unnecessarily," he said. " The price of petrol is really monstrous. But this time we felt it was essential."

" It had happened before?"

" Something of the sort, but this was more serious. We drove in all the likeliest directions, coming back twice to see if she had come in, but saw no sign of her."

" Did you see anything . . .?"

" I know what you are going to ask. Anything that could be connected with poor Parador's death. No, nothing. We were looking only for my sister."

" But you must have passed the Great Ring?"

" We did. It was in the first direction we took. But we noticed nothing unusual. Of course we weren't expecting it."

" No. What time did you give up?"

" It must have been nearly one o'clock. As we both had to be on the train in the morning we could not go on any longer. About an hour later I heard my sister come in. Neither then nor at any time since has she said more than that she had been for a walk. My brother and I are most distressed about it. I trust you won't mind my having told you, a comparative stranger."

" Not in the least. I wish I could be more helpful."

" So you see why I keep a supply of sleeping tablets for my sister."

" She is quite willing to take one when you recommend it?"

" Oh yes. She has been a hospital nurse, you see. She knows the value of these things, used with caution. But my brother would never understand."

" Would you mind telling me how you got them? Was it with a doctor's prescription?"

" No. My sister won't see a doctor if she can help it."

" Then how?"

" I must ask you to treat this in confidence. An employee of ours, I need not mention his name, has some source of supply into which I did not enquire too deeply."

" Is this the first tube he has obtained for you?"

" No. The second."

" Those in the first tube were all used by your sister?"

" I must confess I do occasionally take one myself. But very rarely."

" None were ever missing?"

" None. I keep the key of that cupboard myself."

" Neither you nor your sister ever takes more than one capsule at a time?"

" Never. One is all that is necessary."

Carolus hesitated.

" You know why I ask all these seemingly impertinent questions?" he asked.

" I understand you are connected in some way with an insurance company."

" You don't mind my asking one or two more?"

" It depends on their nature, of course. But I know of nothing I might wish to conceal."

" Your brother and you are the sole proprietors of Placketts, the famous gunshop in Cheapside, I believe?"

" That is so. Our business is not merely in firearms though.

Sporting equipment of every kind. It has become more all-embracing with modern conditions."

"I see. And you are thinking of selling it?"

"Oh no. We are thinking of amalgamating. Ski-Tent, the largest firm in the British Isles are anxious . . . well, it is a highly complicated transaction and I really cannot see that it can be relevant to your enquiries."

"Only in so far as it is relevant to Felix Parador's death," said Carolus.

Edward stared.

"I don't understand you."

"I have reason to think that Parador had acquired some interest in your business."

"Technically, yes. At a certain point we were under-capitalised. If the amalgamation I have mentioned took place he was in a position to realise a very large profit on a comparatively small investment. That is all I can say on that subject, Mr. Deene."

"Thank you for being so frank. You have given me some valuable information."

As they reached the door Nora came in with a laden basket. She scarcely greeted Carolus but passed on, only saying to her brother, "Potatoes have gone up tuppence."

This news seemed to concern Edward more closely than anything he had heard from Carolus.

Chapter Nine

CAROLUS FOUND RUPERT PRIGGLEY IN THE SALOON BAR OF THE Royal Oak. His expression was of extreme disgust if not open fury.

"How did you get on?" asked Carolus brightly.

"A most revolting experience," said Rupert. "Langley Wood was lousy with children."

"Many?"

"Hundreds. Some half-wit had told the vicar's brood he'd give them sixpence a bunch for primroses, and they'd pulled in all the undersized, snotty-nosed, mewling children from miles around. The whole wood was yellow with primroses when we got there. Now it's stripped. It'll cost the moron who set it going a quid or two. That's one consolation. But it wrecked my morning."

"I'm sorry. I thought Elspeth's niece was very nice."

"I haven't had a chance to find out yet with those blasted children." He was staring out of the window. "God! They're coming here."

Carolus looked out and saw an intimidating spectacle. Priggley fortunately had exaggerated numbers somewhat but the vicar's children had been joined by half a dozen friends and every one of them was laden with primroses.

One came to the door.

"We want the man that was at the vicarage this morning," came a stern if treble voice.

Rupert Priggley looked at Carolus.

"So you did that dirty act, did you, sir? You'd better pay them now. I should say they've got about a fiver's worth, off-hand."

Carolus paled.

"How many children are there?" he said. "Never mind the primroses."

"They're increasing every moment." Then moved to pity, he said, "You're safe enough while you stay in here. Gray-Somerset will never allow them on the premises. But you've got to go out some time and they'll tear you in strips."

Carolus went through to the public bar where fortunately he found Boggett, who listened while Carolus explained the situation.

"You leave it to me," said Boggett. Then calculating from the window, he added, "I reckon it'll take a tenner to get you out of this. Safe and sound, I mean. I wouldn't answer for it if they was to catch sight of you."

Carolus handed over the money and was relieved when he saw Boggett, like the Pied Piper, lead the avid crowd a few yards away.

"All those with ten bunches or more over here," he heard.

"What are you going to do with the primroses?" asked Rupert mercilessly.

"Give them to the hosp . . . No? Miss Limp . . . You don't think so? Burn them, then."

"You can't do that, sir. Despoiling the countryside."

"Boggett will think of something," said Carolus.

He was right. After lunch the primroses had disappeared. So had Boggett, with the change from ten pounds.

That afternoon Carolus went to see a man he regarded as

potentially his most important witness. This was William Flood, the car park attendant at the station. He had sought instructions from the barman at the Royal Oak.

"Old Billy Flood? Yes, you'll find him there. You'd think he'd take the time off between the morning trains and when they come down in the evening, wouldn't you? Not him. He's a crafty old sort, is Billy. He doesn't like one of them to get away without paying. See, he gets so much a ticket. He's no fool, either. It's no good their trying to dodge him. He can get across that car park quicker on his one leg than you could do on your two."

"I want to ask him a few questions."

"He'll tell you all right, so long as there's something for him in it."

This, Carolus found, was true. Mr. Flood was small with a puckered face and a look both greedy and cunning. For the first few minutes, while Carolus was explaining what he wanted to know he kept him under keen observation, saying little. Then he took over.

"Let's understand one another," he said. "You want some information from me. Right?"

Carolus nodded.

"And it's information only I can give you. Right. Referring to the day before Mr. Parador was found dead. Right?"

"And the day after," Carolus inserted.

"*And* the day after," conceded Mr. Flood. "Depending on what I remember. Right?"

"Yes. But what *do* you remember?"

"We're coming to that. If I was to tell you I remember everything, every blessed thing, about those two days, who put their cars in and what time and when they took them out, what would you say then?"

"I'd say it was a miracle."

"Ah!" chuckled Mr. Flood. "I know you would. But you'd be wrong. There's no miracle about it. I know my job. And as soon as Mr. Parador didn't come that morning I knew it was Something and took particular note."

"You mean you wrote it down?"

93

" No. In my head I mean. All the times and everything. What do you say to that?"

" I say a fiver," said Carolus.

" And *I* say a tenner," said Mr. Flood triumphantly. " Seeing as you come from the insurance company. I say a tenner or nothing."

Twice in one day, thought Carolus, but agreed.

" Only," went on Mr. Flood, " there's another question here. Are you going to trust me or am I going to trust you? We can't have it both ways."

" I'll give you a fiver first and the rest when you've answered my questions."

" Half and half, eh? I'd sooner you'd said, ' I'll trust you, Flood. I know you wouldn't take money on false pretences, not after you've been in charge of this car park for all these years '. I'd sooner you'd have said that. It would have shown more confidence, like." His little eyes were watching Carolus but when he saw nothing responsive in his face he agreed. " All right," he said. " We'll do it that way."

The five-pound note which Carolus handed him disappeared.

" Now, what's the first?"

" It's about Mr. Parador himself. He went up to town every day at the same time?"

" Very seldom he missed. Very seldom. I can't remember him missing a day since the summer when him and his wife went abroad."

" He drove in from his house alone?"

" That's it. If she went up to town it was later in the day."

" And he arrived about the same time every morning?"

" Always gave himself about ten minutes for the train."

" What about coming down at night?"

" Ah, that you never could say. One day it would be on the train that gets in at four six, another day he might come on the last train at night. But his usual time was on the train arriving at 6.45. Say four times a week he was on that."

" What about on his last night?"

" That's what he came on. The 6.45."

94

"You spoke to him?"

"He spoke to me. ' 'Evening, Flood ', he said, quite cheerful he sounded."

"You could see him clearly?"

"The lights were on. They keep the car park lit at night. See him? I could see him as plain as I see you now."

"Was he carrying anything?"

For the first time Billy Flood hesitated. Then his eye went down to the brief-case in Carolus's hand.

"So that's it, is it? Trying to catch me out! You won't do that so easy. That's what he was carrying. That very case you've got there. He never went up to town without it."

"You're sure he had it on that particular night?"

"Certainly I am. He handed it to me to hold while he unlocked the door of his car."

"Was the train on time that night?"

"No. About twenty minutes behind. By the time he'd got away from the car park I daresay it was seven o'clock."

"Was anyone with him?"

"No. Mr. Rumble came down on the same train but I didn't see them together. Mr. Rumble's car was at the other end of the park. I went over to him after I'd seen Mr. Parador. There wasn't many more on that train. None of what I call the old Brenstead crowd."

"Not Mr. Thriver?"

"No. He was on the five twelve that evening. His daughter came and took the car out in the morning after he'd gone, and brought it back before his train got in. Whether he was to know or not I couldn't say."

"What about the Limpoles?"

Billy Flood looked disgusted.

"I know who you mean, but I don't have nothing to do with them. They don't bring their car to the station. They walk down every day like a couple of mumpers in case it would cost them a few pence in petrol. But Dogman very often leaves his car here. Only She's the danger."

"What d'you mean?"

95

" That day, for instance, she drove him down in the morning, then off she goes in the car and when he got down on the five twelve (same as Thriver), there was no car for him. I suppose she was on the bottle somewhere. Thriver gave him a lift."

" So that's all you saw of any of them that evening?"

" That's it. I went home after the nine fifteen got in, as I always do, and there was nothing left in the park except those in the corner over there whose owners are away."

" So you'd seen everyone off and the park was empty. An evening like any other."

" That's about it. I never noticed anything different till next morning."

" Then?"

" Then, there it was. Mr. Parador didn't arrive. If he'd said anything to me on the previous night I'd have understood it. He knew I always kept his place for him—over in the corner. You'd have thought he'd have said, ' Shan't be going up in the morning ', or something of that."

" But Mr. Flood, this park must hold sixty cars."

" Not quite, it doesn't. Forty-two, the way I have them put."

" How can you possibly remember all of them?"

" I don't. Not all of them. There's some miserable effers don't speak to you at all. One's been parking here five years and never said a word to me even at Christmas time. But you get to know them in a job like this, specially those from what we call Old Brenstead."

" If someone new appears then you would notice it."

" Not always. I can't say that. There's a few you've never seen before and never see again. But very often I do. Why?"

" There was a man on the morning after Mr. Parador's death . . ."

" Yes. I've heard about him. Lot of talk about him there's been. Knew all about it, didn't he? Told them in the compartment where the body was and all that."

" The story has become exaggerated, of course. But a man got into the compartment in which Mr. Parador usually travelled and said he wouldn't be coming."

" Yes, that's what I heard."

" Did you see him that morning?"

Mr. Flood looked even more furtive.

" You want to know a lot, don't you? I can see you're a gentleman that likes his money's worth. Still, fair's fair. I said I'd answer your questions and I will. Yes, I saw him."

" You did?"

" Certainly I did. Came up on a motor-bike about five minutes before the train. Seemed in a bit of a hurry. ' Can I leave it here?' he asked me. I couldn't see what he was like because he had these dark glasses. I showed him where to put his bike and he ran over to the booking office."

" That was the last you saw of him?"

" No, it wasn't. Otherwise his bike would still be here, wouldn't it? He came down again on the slow train. Leaves London at one and gets in at half past two, near enough. I'd just been over to the Station Hotel at the time. Never thought there'd be anyone for the car park off that train. I happened to look out of the window when I see him coming out of the station. Oh, I thought, he wants to get away without paying, does he? So I hopped across."

" Did you get a better view of him, this time?"

" He still had these glasses on. He was on about his motorcycle. How fast it was, and that. Then he began to ask me questions, which is a thing I don't like unless there's anything to it, as you might say. Did the same ones go up together every morning? Did they all come from here? That sort of thing. So I shut him up. I'm paid to look after their cars not to talk about their private lives, I told him. He didn't like that. ' I was only asking ', he said. ' Then you ask someone else ', I told him, ' because I haven't got time to stand about gossiping '. Nor I haven't."

" Of course not. But this time, surely, you must have seen something more of the man?"

" Not much. He was middle height, youngish I should say, and spoke in a deep sort of voice. All dressed in black he was, with a black overcoat, but no motor-cycling things. Something creepy about him, I thought, though of course I knew nothing then."

" What make was his motor-cycle?"

" Criterion. The big kind. Dangerous things, those. He paid for leaving it there and was off."

" In which direction?"

" I didn't notice that. I wasn't to know there was anything about him, was I? I went back to the Station Hotel to finish my drink."

" So you didn't notice his registration number?"

If Mr. Flood had looked shifty before he now became positively Machiavellian.

" I haven't said that, have I? I always take the number down when it's something I haven't see before and wonder whether the driver will try to slip off or not. Yes, I've got his number all right."

Carolus waited.

" Only I shouldn't hardly call giving you that answering questions. It's more like handing something over, isn't it? A number, I mean. That's different."

" Haven't you had to give it to the police?"

" No. Nobody's asked me, till now. It's all forgotten except for me. I don't suppose you'd ever find out what that number was unless I was to tell you."

" No. I don't suppose I should. That's why I'm paying you ten pounds."

There was a limit to extortion, after all.

" I know you are. But a number's a different thing."

" I shouldn't feel our contract had been fulfilled without it," said Carolus gravely.

The full import of this had to be considered carefully by Mr. Flood. " That will be all you want to know if I give it to you?"

" Yes. That's the lot."

" All right. You win."

A number of small pieces of paper were pulled from a pocket and examined.

" Here it is. BYY 018. Now what about The Other?"

Carolus carefully noted down the number, then extracted another five-pound note.

" I reckon you got that cheap," said Mr. Flood.

" You may well be right. Don't answer this if you don't want to, but I'd like to know if you've ever seen that man, or that motor-bike again?"

" No, I haven't. I don't get about much. It's not been back in the park, that's a certainty. If it had I should have noticed it. There's one thing I've often wondered, though. What did he go up to London for that day? That's what I'd like to know. He couldn't have had more than an hour up there, could he?"

" I suppose not."

" And he went first-class."

Just then they were both startled by the sound of a powerful motor-cycle approaching rapidly from the main road. A Criterion was being ridden into the park.

" This looks like it," said Mr. Flood.

" No," said Carolus regretfully, for he had seen the rider.

It was Priggley.

" Hullo, sir. I've just bought this piece of ironmongery," he said.

" Have you got a driving licence?"

Priggley grinned.

" You talk like the Law. Yes, I have. Daddy bought me a motor-bike last year to get me out of the house when he was having that affair with an Austrian girl. He said he hoped I'd break my neck on it. I had to sell it because a horse let me down badly in the Derby. But this is a neater job altogether."

Carolus noticing that the registration number had nothing in common with the one he had written down said, " Where did you get it?"

" It belonged to Bert Holey, the man who owns the filling station. Or rather to his son. His wife didn't like him having it because she thought it dangerous and he hasn't insured his life yet. So I got it for virtually nothing. It has only done a couple of thousand and he took twenty-five per cent off the price new."

" It doesn't sound cheap to me. And I doubt if your parents would approve."

" Why not? What have they got to lose?"

"There is that," agreed Carolus. "I didn't know you had so much money."

"This was hush money from mummy's new lover. He's a Texan and understands the sort of thing a young man needs. I've shown it to Bunty. She seems to approve but I must own she's pretty dumb. Shapely, yes, but stupid. She said, 'Does it go very fast?' I ask you. I wanted her to try it but she says she's got to be in at tea-time. Some dreary man's coming to see her aunt."

"Yes," said Carolus looking at his watch. "I must be going."

"Oh, it's you. I'll come with you, then. Pick me up at the Oak, will you? I'll put this in the garage there and we can go sedately in the Bentley."

"Insufferable little mountebank," said Carolus.

"Well," said Mr. Flood when Rupert had gone. "That's a fly one, isn't he?"

"I'm afraid you're right," said Carolus.

Chapter Ten

FROM THE ROAD THE OLD MANOR LOOKED ENCHANTING. THERE were great trees behind it and on both sides so that its double row of long Georgian windows facing the road must be the only ones visible from any distance, and they stared out from a Georgian façade towards the south. Admirable planning, particularly as the house stood back far enough to prevent anyone seeing into the rooms from the lane. No outbuildings were visible but when he drove in Carolus saw that the drive continued along the north end of the house to a great courtyard at the back, and that the stables here had been converted into garages. He left the car in the courtyard where most of the daylight had faded; so thick were the surrounding trees that from here the place seemed like a house in a forest.

The front door was opened by Elspeth herself.

"Please let's use first names," she said when they had greeted one another with formality. "I long to say Carolus. It's a charming name. Come into the fire. Bunty's making tea."

It was all very English, furniture, decoration, atmosphere. If there had been a footman or a maid in a stiff apron it would have belonged to a world which neither Carolus nor Elspeth was quite old enough to remember. The curtains were drawn, the fire blazed and the lighting was soft and cosy. When Bunty appeared with a silver tray and they were given tea and toast a tranquillity seemed to descend on them and even Carolus showed no eagerness to ask questions. They made small talk, Rupert telling the story of the primroses, and Bunty, a literal-minded girl, wondered what *had* happened to the flowers.

Elspeth went out with the tray and Rupert quickly said to Bunty, " Haven't you some tame rabbits or something to show me?"

" Rabbits? No, of course not."

" Well, *something*," said Rupert desperately.

" Oh, I see. Oh yes. We could go and play table-tennis."

" That'll do," said Rupert hurriedly and they left.

" Now," said Elspeth when she returned, " we can have that good old talk. You know, I feel I can tell you anything. Not that there's much to tell."

Carolus, who had brought the brief-case in with him, found it had failed to register, even when he took some papers out of it, said, " D'you want me to ask the questions?"

" Oh yes, please. If I wander from the point you must drag me back."

" First of all, did your husband really believe he had cancer?"

" That's rather hard to answer. He had an idea he had at one time, but I'd heard no more about it for ages. It wasn't really that he quarrelled with Dr. Sporlott over it, at least not directly. He heard that Sporlott had made a remark, something like ' poor old Parador, thinks he's got cancer '. He felt this was a breach of confidence more than anything else and never spoke to Sporlott again. He hated any sort of breach of confidence."

" Sporlott told me they had a row but did not go into the details."

" I don't think there was an open row. Felix just changed his doctor. I like Sporlott, though. He takes care of his *old* patients and that's a good thing. Felix went to Kumar Shant after that. Over at Buttsfield."

" When did this happen?"

" I should think about six months ago."

" Did he consult the Indian doctor frequently?"

" Pretty often. He was a bit of an old fusspot about his health. He drove over to see him the night before he died, actually. That was the Wednesday. I know because he gave me a prescription to take to Scotter. Scotter thought it might be for heartburn. I asked him when I took the prescription in."

" That would be on the morning of Thursday. The day . . ."

" Yes, Carolus. The day he died. I got the pills. Buscapine, they were called. But of course he never took any. The police took charge of the bottle which was not opened."

" I see. Anyway, you don't think it was fear of cancer which caused him to . . ."

" No, I don't. I'm sure he'd have told me if he was worried about it. He didn't keep things from me. At least . . ."

" You're thinking of that woman last night."

" Of course I am. How can I help it? It was so *ghastly*."

" I thought you behaved splendidly."

Elspeth smiled. " I'm probably bitchier than you think. I knew she was trying to humiliate me. I tried to carry it off, but I'm afraid I broke down afterwards. You see, I knew her of old. I introduced them, but I never dreamt . . . Even now I can't believe it quite. There may have been something between them once, but I'm sure he wasn't . . . keeping her."

" D'you know where she lives?"

" She used to live in London. Some mews, somewhere. She was on the stage for years. Never anything big but she made a living. At first I thought she was just drunk. Then I realised it was calculated."

" She was thrown out," said Carolus consolingly.

" I know. But that doesn't really help. You know it's beastly to find all of a sudden that there's someone who hates you. However, you can't want to know about Henrietta Ballard. What can I tell you that's useful?"

" I liked the way Rumble came to your assistance."

" Jimmy? Oh, he's a pet."

103

" If I knew you better and had any excuse for it I'd ask if you . . ."

" If I am in love with him? No. Not yet. I know it seems too awful just after Felix and everything, but I am getting fond of Jimmy Rumble."

" And he's in love with you."

" Think so?" smiled Elspeth.

" I'm sure of it."

" We're going down another blind alley. *Do* ask some sensible questions."

" Right. I will. Your husband was writing his memoirs?"

" Yes. He had a very interesting life, you know. He was in Intelligence in the Far East for years."

" How much could he say about that?"

" That was the point. I don't think he knew quite. He'd taken all sorts of oaths. Apparently even *years* afterwards you can't say what you like. Young Patsy was quite worried about it. Anyway, the police took away all his papers. I understand the book had been read before the inquest. To see if it threw any light, you know. But it seemed there was nothing. He hadn't reached the war yet, and said very little about himself. He wasn't a bit of an egotist, you know."

"' I wonder why he wanted to write it."

" Why *do* people write books? I told him he was crazy to shut himself away on lovely fine days, writing away at something that might never be read. But he wanted to finish it, he said."

" Patsy Thriver was glad to do it?"

" I expect he paid her very well. I didn't ask. It was pocket-money for her. I don't suppose her father is over-generous."

" Strange man, that. He told me he came here that . . . Thursday night."

" He did. I was just going to bed. He didn't know Felix hadn't come down."

" He was an old friend of the family?"

" Of Felix and Magnus, yes. He wasn't really a friend of mine. I mean, I had nothing against him. But they'd all been boys together. He rang up today, by the way."

" Yes?"

" It's about Felix's will. You know I haven't even seen it, yet. I know what it says so far as I'm concerned and that's all I can bear just now. Felix always told me it was all for me and Magnus. Mostly for me. Thriver says that's still the sense of it. But he wants to talk to me about it. There's some hitch or something. He's coming in tomorrow."

" Then you'll know how many of your husband's quarrels went deep."

" Oh, I hope none of them. Those poor Hopeladys, for instance. He wouldn't have . . . All over a silly little incident."

" I don't know. I've known worse reasons for cutting someone out of a will."

" Yes, but they're so poor. And all those children. If he has I shall have to do something. Of course, the vicar's infuriating. But he doesn't really mean any harm. His poor little wife's always having to stick up for him."

" He was out in his car that Thursday night," said Carolus flatly.

Elspeth looked genuinely surprised.

" *Was* he?"

" Going to see a dying parishioner, he told me. A Mrs. Grantham."

" Oh yes. But she'd been ill for ages. She didn't die till some days later."

There was a long silence.

" Carolus," said Elspeth at last, " you don't think that if Felix did cut anyone out they might . . . no, it's too far-fetched."

" I never make guesses like that. If I do, I never admit to them."

" They are such a strange lot here, you see. Look at Enid Thriver. You'd think she was not all there sometimes. But she can be as shrewd as anyone when she wants to. Then those Limpoles. Felix had some business with them which I never quite understood."

" I haven't met Charles Limpole yet."

" He's the worst. No, not worst, I don't mean that. He's the narrower one of the two."

" So I've heard."

" What do you think of Dogman?"

" I've scarcely spoken to him."

" I like her," continued Elspeth. " I'm sorry for her, too. There must be something that makes her drink like that."

Carolus refused to be drawn.

" I suppose I like almost everybody, really," said Elspeth. " Though I must own I find Scotter a bit hard to take."

" Yes. A rather extraordinary man," said Carolus, making one of those banal comments which so often lead to enlargement of the other's theme.

" Felix used to know his father years ago. He was a red-hot socialist in the days before there were many. A carpenter by trade, I believe, but known around here as a rebel-rouser. Our Scotter's torn between loyalty to his father and his own social ambitions. He idolised his father, I believe, and was a boy of twelve when he found out that he had died in a Japanese prisoner-of-war camp."

" All that may account for his defensiveness."

" Yes, but it's so difficult. I don't think we're a bit snobbish in this town, but Scotter seems to do his best to make us. He's asked everywhere—he's a very good bridge player—but he's so class conscious one feels uncomfortable."

" But an efficient chemist?"

" Oh yes. I should think *very*. I am giving you all the gossip, aren't I? But I suppose it's important or you wouldn't make me chatter."

" How do you like Boggett?"

" You know," said Elspeth, smiling as though she thought she were giving him a surprise, " I *like* Boggett. He's an old villain, of course, and as lazy as sin, but there's something about him. Felix used to get terribly exasperated with him, but as I told him he would never get anyone else to work in the garden. Not that he did much work, but it was something. Felix said he only came to pick up his wages. He sacked him once."

" So I heard."

" Boggett turned up after lunch one day terribly drunk and tried to cut the lawn. It was rather pathetic really. I persuaded Felix to take him back. Have you seen Mrs. Boggett? She works for Jimmy Rumble. She's twice the worker Boggett is. Don't you think it's time we had a drink?"

Carolus did. He had heard almost as much as he wanted of local tittle-tattle, but there was one thing more he intended to ask.

" I want to come back to Hopelady for a moment, if you don't mind."

" Oh, poor Hopelady. He's a simple soul."

" You think so? He came here on that Thursday afternoon, I believe?"

There was no need to explain which Thursday. But Elspeth was puzzled for a moment.

" Did he? Yes, so he did."

" Any particular reason?"

" Yes. I'm afraid it was the usual. He wanted money for something. He hoped I could put things right between him and Felix. They really are very poor."

" You mean he wanted to borrow money? For himself or his family?"

" That's what it came to, really. Felix had lent him money before, you see. Well, given it would be more accurate. You can't blame Hopelady. I can't think why he's not paid sufficiently."

" Did you give him any?"

" No. Not that time. I really couldn't, you know, without persuading Felix. I said I'd try to do that but I really hadn't any to spare. Of my own, I mean. He was a bit crestfallen but I told him I would do what I could."

" Did you see him again—until last night?"

" Oh yes. He was at the inquest, I think. Then, of course, he buried Felix." The voice grew restrained. " I suppose I ought to be thankful they've done away with that ' unhallowed ground ' wickedness. Anyway, I saw poor Hopelady at the funeral. He's a bag of nerves, really. All that practical joking is the result of nerves, I'm sure of it. Where do you think our children have got to?"

With more feeling than seemed necessary Carolus said, "I should hate to guess."

Elspeth went to the door and called "Bunty!" several times without result.

"Haven't you a fire alarm or something you can set in motion?" asked Carolus.

After a few moments, however, the two appeared, Rupert as cool as usual, Bunty a trifle ruffled.

"Wherever were you?" asked Elspeth.

"Bunty was showing me her needlework," said Rupert.

Elspeth did not lose her good humour and Carolus and Rupert went round to the car and drove off.

"Is that child *dumb*?" asked Rupert rhetorically. "Hullo, what's this?" For standing in the drive facing them was a car with sidelights on.

Carolus pulled up and waited till the driver of the car came to his window. It was James Rumble.

"I thought it was you, Deene. Have you been bothering Elspeth with questions?"

Carolus could see that the man was choking with anger.

"Yes," he said simply.

"Then I'm going to tell you that I won't have it. She's been through quite enough already. You have no possible right to worry her any more. None!"

"Don't get hysterical," said Carolus. "Mrs. Parador asked me to come and see her."

"Because her conceited ass of a brother-in-law asked her to. Can't you see she doesn't know which way to turn? What do you think she must feel, an autopsy on her husband's body, an inquest, haven't you any feelings? Can't you realise what she's been through?"

"I can. Yes," said Carolus. "But unfortunately the truth isn't reached without some disturbance of people's feelings. As a matter of fact I think you will find Elspeth feels better for telling me all she has."

"I very much doubt it. She wants to forget the whole nightmare. I know she does. The verdict has been given . . ."

"Listen, Rumble. Tell me honestly. Do *you* think Felix Parador committed suicide?"

Rumble tried to answer, mouthing his words. Then, almost shouting, he said, "What's that to do with it? I tell you I won't have her pestered in this way. She is just beginning to get over the ghastly business and you come along delving into it, upsetting her. I won't stand for it. I'm telling you, if you go on like this you'll have me to reckon with. You can question whoever you like, do what you like, but I won't have Elspeth upset."

Carolus was not provoked to an angry retort. On the contrary he spoke with some sympathy.

"I know what you feel," he said. "But you're mistaken, I assure you. I have done nothing to upset Mrs. Parador. It's only you who are 'upset', as you put it. Go up and see her and you will find that what I tell you is true. Now please back your car and let me get past."

Rumble hesitated, then began to turn away.

"Don't forget what I've said," he suddenly shouted back. "I mean every word of it."

Then he got into his car and started, rather inexpertly, to back towards the gate.

"Highly-strung character," commented Priggley.

"The man's in love."

"Oh, don't talk like a Victorian novel, sir. It's so morbid. I see what you mean, though. Think he'll give any more trouble?"

"No. She'll cool him down."

"Did you learn all you wanted?"

"Yes. I've finished with what is called interrogation."

"Thank God for that. Let's go and have a drink."

The saloon bar of The Royal Oak was empty but for Mr. Gray-Somerset who was thoughtfully filing his nails.

"You didn't tell me," he said when he had served their drinks, "that you were some kind of detective. I could probably have been helpful to you. I've rather a flair for that sort of thing. M.I. you know for a number of years."

109

"You must have had lots to talk about with Felix Parador then."

"Not really. Different branch. Mine was very hush hush stuff."

"Atomic research?" suggested Carolus.

The idea was evidently irresistible to Mr. Gray-Somerset.

"That sort of thing," he agreed. "I happen to speak Russian."

Carolus made a series of semi-articulate sounds.

"Ah. I see you do, too. Excellent. But about this man Parador. I rather doubt if he *was* M.I. Between ourselves I thought there was something rather phony about him, to be honest."

"Did he come in here much?"

"Here? No. I met him at Gerry Petersfield's."

"Does Lord Petersfield live near here?"

"No. No. No. This was some time ago. Gerry's a distant relation of mine. He agreed with me about Parador. Not quite ' right ' he said. I've thought of it since this thing happened. I met a lot of phonies when I was in the Congo. Seemed to collect there."

"Really?"

"Definitely. But I had an interesting job there, Security sort of thing, only more on the active side. I was talking about it once to Dogman when a most extraordinary thing happened. He suddenly jumped up and said, ' I don't want to hear anything about Security. Understand? I don't want to hear the word '. I said it was quite an ordinary word and he shouted, ' Well, don't use it to me '. Then he walked out of the bar. What do you make of that?"

"Interesting," said Carolus. "Has he been in here since?"

"Oh yes. Often. Soon forgot all about it. He once bought a horse I used to own. I lost a packet on that one. Picked it up later on the St. Leger."

"Do you know the vicar?" asked Carolus.

"The vicar? Here, you mean? Hopelady? No! I've just seen him. Keeps the rival establishment down the road. He'd be surprised if he knew how many customers we have in common."

"You don't subscribe to any of his charities, then?"

"No," said Gray-Somerset sharply. "Not in my line."

Chapter Eleven

"I WANT TO USE THAT MOTOR-CYCLE OF YOURS FOR A FEW minutes tomorrow morning," Carolus told Rupert.

"I didn't know you could ride a motor-cycle."

"Yes. One of the few things I learned in the army. Mind if I do that?"

"It's insured," said Rupert ungraciously.

"I have to be up early. Suppose you meet me at the Great Ring at ten o'clock?"

"Look, sir, *don't* be mysterious, please. Is this part of your so-called investigation?"

"It is. Quite an important part."

"OK then."

"Don't say OK," said Carolus with pedantic fretfulness. "You know I detest the expression. There are perfectly good English equivalents. I don't mind Americanisms when they have particular force, as many of them have, but . . ."

"You've got something on your mind. That kind of irritability always means there's something brewing. But all right, then, I'll meet you at the Great Ring at ten."

Carolus rose at seven and by twenty past eight was sitting in his car in the parking place by the station. Billy Flood hobbled across. "What do you want to know this time?" he asked with a greedy twinkle.

"Nothing, Mr. Flood. I just want to watch the departure of the commuters."

"The big lot's gone on the 8.12," he said. "You'll have to wait for the 8.52 now. That's the train most of this lot take," he said, indicating his half-empty car park.

He was called to see a newly-arrived car into place.

"C'm'on, c'm'on, c'm'on, c'm'on," he said. "Bit farther, c'm'on, c'm'on . . ." Crash. The car had hit the low wall. "That'll do," said Mr. Flood, his duty accomplished.

"What about my bumper?" asked the driver furiously.

"What are bumpers for?" asked Mr. Flood, making out his ticket. "I like to get them close up to the wall," he explained to Carolus. "Looks tidier that way."

It was fifteen minutes before the arrival of anyone Carolus knew by sight, but in the meantime an almost continuous stream was arriving at the station, more female than male, he noted. It was thirty years since, as a preparatory schoolboy on holiday, he had seen his father off to the city on a morning train and he was interested by the changes, superficial though they were, in the scene. Less bowlers, less headgear altogether, more brief-cases, less baskets of produce, as many neatly rolled umbrellas. But there was the same rather uncommunicative manner, the same intentness on the matter in hand.

Thriver's car drew up driven by Patsy, and the solicitor got out, apparently without saying a word to his daughter. Patsy saw him and waved her hand as she drove away. Then up the road came Edward Limpole on foot accompanied by a taller, sterner man whom Carolus assumed to be his elder brother Charles. Not a word passed between them as they strode side-by-side to the station entrance and disappeared.

"There's a pair for you," said Mr. Flood. "Tramping down all that way to save paying for parking. It makes you wonder, doesn't it?"

112

"No," said Carolus. "They want the exercise, perhaps."

"Exercise! They wouldn't want exercise if it cost money. Here's Mr. Rumble coming. He'll park in here near you. Or always has done."

Rumble drove in without seeing Carolus, then catching sight of him, came across.

"I owe you an apology, Deene," he said hurriedly. "You were quite right. Elspeth was glad you looked in. I can't wait now but I had to just tell you."

"That's all right," said Carolus cordially.

The pedestrians were beginning to hurry as they entered the station now. How did women manage to walk fast in stiletto heels, he wondered idly. Then he saw Dogman who parked quite near him.

Dogman took trouble to see his car was locked and all the windows up.

"If anyone comes for it," he told Flood, "say it's broken down. Won't start."

"You've locked it, anyway."

"I know, but there might be a duplicate key. I don't think there is but there might be. It's not to leave here, anyway."

"OK," said Flood, and Carolus shuddered.

The train left on time. Carolus gave Flood a couple of half-crowns and drove away. He had seen all he needed.

He reached the Great Ring well before ten o'clock but Priggley was already there.

"Why choose this God-forsaken place?" he asked. "There isn't a soul about."

"That's what I hoped," said Carolus. "Now we will proceed to Operation Smash-up."

"What d'you mean?" asked Priggley anxiously.

"Don't be alarmed."

Carolus instead of putting the Bentley as Mr. Flood would have liked it at right-angles to the edge of the tarmac to form the first of a line of parked cars, had stopped it well out in the open space.

"Now let me try that thing."

"I don't like this a bit," said Rupert. "I don't know what you're up to but I don't like it."

"Just repeat the *Arab's Farewell To His Steed*, then. 'My beautiful, my beautiful, that standeth proudly by . . .'"

Carolus mounted the Criterion and examined it critically.

"Shan't be a moment," he said and rode out of the car park. Rupert could hear him accelerating up the road, then changing down, then returning. He entered the car park apparently in complete control but as he approached the Bentley quite slowly he seemed to lose his head, and coming up on its right side too close, badly gashed its wing and nearly went over.

"Are you mad, sir?" shouted Priggley running forward. "Look what you've done! And what about my bike?"

"Examine it," said Carolus curtly.

"And the Bentley. What on earth happened to you?"

"It *is* a bit of a dent, isn't it?" said Carolus complacently.

"Dent! My God! It will never be the same again."

"You'd be surprised what can be done by a good body-builder. But I think it's convincing, don't you?"

"I suppose you're going to ask me to believe you did that on purpose?"

"I don't ask you to believe anything. In fact the less you believe the better. What I ask you to do is keep your mouth shut. If I couldn't trust you to do that I wouldn't have brought you here."

"It's the last time I get mixed up with one of your lunacies, sir. I really think your mental age must be sixteen or so."

"Now I want you to go back to Newminster. I'll follow you as soon as I can. I'll have your things packed and bring them with me. But don't go back through Brenstead. You can take that to Wayland's garage and get them to check up on it at my expense, but I don't think it's come to any harm."

Rupert stared at him.

"What *is* all this?"

"Tell the Sticks I'll be over as soon as I can."

"I shall be delighted, sir. To tell you the truth I feel as though I'm escaping from a dangerous lunatic."

" I'm not altogether sure you're not. Off you go."

Carolus watched him ride away then started to drive back to Brenstead. It was half past eleven when he reached the police station.

He found Police Officer Brophy behind the counter, looking important.

" Can I see the sergeant in charge?"

Carolus spoke politely enough but his words found no favour with Police Officer Brophy.

" I am the Police Officer in charge," said Police Officer Brophy.

" So I see. But as this is rather a serious matter?"

" The plain clothes lot's all out," said Police Officer Brophy, with not very well concealed disgust. " If that's what you want."

" No, I don't think I need trouble them."

" Then what do you want?"

" I want to report an accident."

" Traffic?"

" You could call it that."

Police Officer Brophy picked up some papers beside him and prepared to take notes.

" Your full name and address, please," he said severely.

" What time will the sergeant be back?"

Police Officer Brophy took this as a challenge.

" If you wish to report an accident I shall be glad to take particulars," he said.

" Thank you, but . . ."

" Perhaps you want to see the Chief Superintendent? Or the Chief Constable?" he suggested sarcastically. " You don't think yours is the only accident on the roads, do you? Now please give me your name and address and we won't waste any more time."

Carolus was about to do so when the door opened behind him and a tall man with a sergeant's insignia and sharp, narrow eyes in a pale blue-chinned face entered.

" What's this, Brophy?" he asked sharply.

" Traffic accident, sir," said Police Officer Brophy.

" Anything serious?" the sergeant asked Carolus.

" Yes. The other party failed to stop," said Carolus.

115

" Why didn't you tell me?" he asked Brophy. " I'll take particulars." He passed behind the counter and Brophy disappeared.
" Now then, sir. Is that your car outside?"

" Yes."

" I made a cursory examination of the damage as I came in," said Sergeant Beckett. " What happened?"

Carolus decided to enter into the spirit of the thing.

" I was proceeding along the Buttsfield road . . ."

Sergeant Beckett nodded as though delighted with the word.
" Time?"

Carolus became vague.

" It must have been about ten," he said. " Or it may have been earlier."

" You didn't notice the exact time?" said Sergeant Beckett with some disappointment.

" No, not exactly."

" Should have done, sir. It's always helpful to have the exact time in these cases. What was your speed?"

" About thirty miles an hour," said Carolus.

Sergeant Beckett sighed.

" You'd be surprised how often cars are travelling at about thirty miles an hour," he said. " Whenever we have to investigate an accident it's always about thirty miles an hour they're travelling. Sure you weren't going faster?"

" If I had been the fellow would have been killed."

" We'll come to that," said Sergeant Beckett ambiguously.
" You were proceeding along the Buttsfield road at approximately thirty miles an hour. Yes?"

" I became aware that a man on a motor-cycle was anxious to pass me . . ."

" Steady now. Steady. *How* did you become aware?"

" In my driving mirror."

" I see. Did you take any note of his appearance or manner of dress?"

" None at all, I'm afraid."

" Pity that. You should always note the appearance and manner of dress."

116

" But I didn't know . . ."

" Never mind then, sir," said Sergeant Beckett forgivingly.

" He came up . . .".

" On your off side?"

" Naturally. And in passing me scraped my offside wing . . ."

" Whoa. Whoa. What made him do that? Anything coming in the opposite direction?"

" Nothing. He just misjudged the distance, I suppose."

" Very unusual that. Unless . . ." The sergeant's eyes brightened. " Unless he was driving under the influence of alcohol."

" I should scarcely think so, at ten o'clock in the morning. But of course I have no means of judging. The impact with my car seemed to be slight, but I could feel it and saw the motor-cyclist swerve and nearly overturn."

" What do you mean by ' nearly overturn '?"

" He looked as though he was going to. But he righted himself and rode on."

" Ah."

" I sounded my horn . . ."

" Sufficiently, you think?"

" Quite sufficiently. I made the hell of a noise. But the motorcyclist seemed only to accelerate."

" You took his number, of course?"

The sergeant looked anxiously at Carolus.

" I tried to. I took a number. But he was moving fast now."

" So you can't swear to the number you took being accurate?"

" Not absolutely for certain."

The sergeant looked superior.

" It's no good taking a number when you're not absolutely certain," he said loftily.

" I'm pretty certain. I said I couldn't swear to it. I regard an oath a serious thing."

" So we all do," said the sergeant unctuously. " Anyway, you took *a* number. Did you write it down?"

" Yes. I stopped immediately and wrote it down. Here it is."

The sergeant studied it carefully.

" BYY 018," he said. " I suppose we shall have to do the best we can with this. Now, were there any witnesses of the accident?"

"None that I know of."

"No passing vehicles?"

"Not for some minutes, I think."

"No one who might be able to identify this motor-cyclist? No? That's unfortunate. It's always best to have the testimony of a third party."

"I'm sorry," said Carolus, who was getting tired of this game. "I'll try to arrange it another time."

"There's no need to be sarcastic, sir. I was only saying that a case like this is easier to deal with when you are able to name one or more independent witnesses. Now may I see your driving licence and insurance certificate?"

Carolus produced them.

"Thank you, sir. What steps did you take to report the accident at the first possible moment?"

"I reversed at the road running up to the Great Ring, which was about a hundred yards ahead of where the accident happened, and came here to report it."

"Quite right. There is no other information you are able to give us?"

"None, I'm afraid."

"It's not very satisfactory, is it? We shall have to trace this number and ascertain if possible whether this motor-cycle could have been in the vicinity at the time stated."

"Exactly. Will that take long, do you think?"

"It doesn't depend on us," said Sergeant Beckett. "It has to go through the proper channels. We've had cases like this before where the complainant has not been able to give us satisfactory details. But the matter will receive immediate attention. Have you an address in this neighbourhood?"

"I'm staying at The Royal Oak."

"I see. You expect to be there for some days?"

"Till this has been settled, yes."

"Very good, sir. We will take the necessary steps and let you know at the first moment possible."

"Good. Mind telling me your name so that I may know who is in charge of the investigation?"

"It's not usual but I see no reason against my telling you. Sergeant Beckett is my name."

Carolus rose to go but the sergeant raised a restraining hand.

"We haven't quite finished yet," he said. "I must ask you to indicate the supposed site of the accident."

"But there were no marks or anything," said Carolus.

"Better let Us judge of that, don't you think, sir? We are not without experience in these cases. We shall wish to take measurements."

"Of what?" asked Carolus innocently.

"It's a matter of procedure. Now if you will accompany me in the police car?"

"I'd prefer to drive my own. I was on my way to Buttsfield when this happened."

"Very well, sir. There is no objection to that. It would be best if you preceded us and stopped just short of where you calculate the accident took place."

Carolus led the way to his car and Sergeant Beckett with another man prepared to follow him in a police car.

"Take it easy now, sir," the sergeant warned. "We don't want to pinch *you* for speeding in a built-up area."

He passed the Three Thistles and about three hundred yards from the turning which led to the Great Ring Carolus pulled up and waited.

"Must have been about here," he told Sergeant Beckett when he arrived.

"This is where the incident occurred is it? How near would you say you were from the kerb?"

"Oh, the usual distance. A yard or four feet."

"And from the crown of the road?"

"Perhaps another yard."

"This is all very unsatisfactory, isn't it? Now exactly to what point had you arrived when the motor-cyclist attempted to pass you?"

119

"I've no idea. When I stopped I was a couple of hundred yards or so short of the turning."

The sergeant shook his head sadly and turned to his assistant.

"No skid marks?" he said.

"Nothing visible to the naked eye," said the man in the same jargon.

"You say the motor-cyclist nearly overturned. Where would you say he was in relation to the kerb when that took place?"

"Some way out, I should say. It seemed to send him out across the road."

"Fortunate there was nothing coming in the other direction," commented the sergeant.

"I thought you said that was unfortunate because we needed a witness?"

"You know very well what I mean," said Sergeant Beckett, and indeed Carolus did.

Chapter Twelve

CAROLUS WAS CALLED TO THE TELEPHONE THAT EVENING AND AT once recognised Thriver's high-pitched voice.

" I'd like to see you, Deene," he said curtly.

" I'll be at the Oak all the evening if you'd like to come round."

Thriver sounded distressed.

" It's a very confidential matter," he said. " I hoped you would come round here."

" Very well. I'll be round in a few minutes. But I shall have to hurry back as I'm expecting someone here."

It was a bore, he thought. But when he reached Thriver's study and heard what the solicitor had to say, he changed his mind.

" Most extraordinary thing has happened," piped Thriver. " The will, Parador's will! It came to my office. Through the post. Unregistered. Just like an ordinary letter."

" Any enclosure?"

" None."

" You kept the envelope, of course?"

" One of my clerks opened it. Unfortunately before I reached the office it had been thrown away."

" Where was the postmark?"

" Hickey did not notice. He had perhaps forty or fifty letters to open. But surely the important thing is that we have it back."

" The important thing is—who sent it back?"

" The thief, of course. The man who stole Felix's brief-case from the car that night. He realised that this was no good to him so decided to post it back."

" How would he have known your address?"

" It was in one of our envelopes with the name of the firm and the address die-stamped on the flap of the envelope."

" I'm a bit sceptical about benevolent thieves. Especially some weeks after the event."

" At least it clears up a problem for me. I can now see Magnus, who is the executor, and go ahead."

" Yes, I can see it saves you embarrassment. You have told me all the beneficiaries, haven't you?"

" I think so, yes."

" Does any member of your own family receive anything?"

" I thought you understood that. Yes, there is a token to me . . ."

" A token?"

" Five thousand pounds. And a thousand to my daughter. We were school friends, you see."

" Quite. Did you want to tell me anything else?"

" No. Just that. I thought you should know."

" You will have to see Henrietta Ballard, I take it?"

" I shall write to her. She lives in Buttsfield."

When Carolus got back to The Royal Oak he found Dogman in the saloon bar fairly drunk. There was no sign of his wife.

" Evening, Deene," he greeted Carolus. " Come'n have a drink. Never had a chance to talk to you the other night. Too many people. You're investigating I hear? Yes, needed investigation. Parador wasn't the man for suicide. Too self-centred. Thought too much of himself. I've known him a long time. Well,

122

ever since I came to live here. Soon after the war."

"You didn't know him before that?"

"Never seen him in my life till I came to live here. I was in the army. Parador was never in the army. N'telligence, yes; not the army. But the Japs got him. They got everyone out there, you know. Everyone. Same whoever you were. It should have been. Not nice, Deene. Not nice at all. No one bothered then about how a man died. Or why. Different now. I travelled in the train with him every day. Used to sit there doing the cross-word puzzle. You'd never have thought he'd been through anything. Same with me. Wife always says its left a mark on me. S'nonsense. It was damned unpleasant but so are a lot of things. Don't want to talk about that. Forgotten now, or it ought to be. Yes, I'll have a gin and ginger ale."

Carolus waited for more, but Dogman was now addressing Gray-Somerset.

"You were never in a Jap prisoner-of-war camp, were you? That's one place you haven't been."

"I was very near it," began the landlord. "I just . . ."

"Don't give me that. You can say what you bloody well like. You were Emperor of Japan, if you like. I don't care what you were. But don't tell me you were a Jap prisoner-of-war. You wouldn't be so pleased with yourself if you had been." Dogman turned back to Carolus. "Yes, I knew Parador well. Ran an account with me. Not a great racing man but when he did have a bet it was a big one. D'you follow racing at all? No? Sensible fellow. S'the hell of a life. Up one minute, down the next. You better have another drink. Somerset closes on the dot, don't you, Somerset? Right on the dot. Ah well. Cheery-ho."

It was not until two mornings later that Carolus received the summons he was expecting. He had just finished breakfast and was going out to his car when he saw Police Officer Brophy standing near it.

"I was waiting for you," said the police officer, rather sourly.

"Really? Why didn't you come in?"

"My instructions were to catch you as you came out. Police

Sergeant Beckett would like to see you at once. 'Police Officer Brophy', he said to me, 'go round and tell Mr. Deene, staying at the Oak, to come round here immediately', he said."

"I hope he's got the information I want."

"He's got something, but what it is I don't know. He's in a nasty mood this morning. I don't know why he couldn't telephone. Anyway, there you are. I've told you."

"Yes, thank you, Police Officer Brophy."

As he drove to the local police station Carolus passed Brophy cycling stolidly along in the same direction. He found Sergeant Beckett in a somewhat excited state.

"This is a nice thing, Mr. Deene," he began at once.

"What's the matter? Couldn't you find the motor-cycle?"

"We've found the motor-cycle!" he said, raising his voice almost to a shout. "We've found it all right. Only it's not the motor-cycle."

"I don't quite follow," said Carolus.

Sergeant Beckett made an impatient noise.

"You came here with a story about your car having been run into by a motor-cycle and the driver not stopping. What's more you gave us the number of that motor-cycle. We trace that number. And what do we find? We find that motor-cycle belongs to a gentleman in Buttsfield—a Mr. George Catford."

"Well, there you are. It was on the road to Buttsfield."

"We're not there at all. That motor-cycle, the one you gave us the number of, couldn't have been out on the road that morning because it had been in pieces for three days at a garage in the town being decarbonised and I don't know what else. Our people have seen the garage proprietor who is a thoroughly trustworthy man and is prepared to swear to it, him and three of his staff, that at the time in question it was in his garage in a dozen pieces or more. What do you say to that?"

"Strange," said Carolus.

"Strange, you call it? And the owner of the motor-cycle never went out of where he's staying, where they let rooms, Rosehurst, Brenstead Road, till he left on foot for the estate agent's where he works, five minutes away, arriving there five minutes later and staying there all the morning with half a dozen witnesses to prove it."

" Oh dear. I must have been mistaken, then."

Sergeant Beckett looked at him severely.

" Yes. But there's something funny about this, Mr. Deene. Something very funny. You come to us with a number . . ."

" Mistaken, evidently."

" Of a motor-cycle which belongs to a local man. The number's accurate enough, there it is—BYY 018, but it's not the cycle that did the damage because it's under repairs."

" Coincidence," murmured Carolus, who had the information he required, and wanted to be off.

" It's a funny sort of coincidence, isn't it? The very number, right down to the last digit. You couldn't have been trying to get anyone in trouble, could you, Mr. Deene?"

" Certainly not. I've never seen any George Catford. I simply want the man who damaged my car."

" Then what made you give us Mr. Catford's number?"

" That's what it looked like to me," said Carolus. " I said I couldn't swear to it."

" I wouldn't have taken any notice," said the sergeant, " if it hadn't been the number of a motor-cycle in the district. That's what gives the case a highly questionable aspect."

This, thought Carolus, was where we came in.

" I must be running along," he said. " I'm sorry you haven't been able to find the motor-cycle which did the damage, but of course it's partly my fault. I must have made a mistake about the number. Ah well. It won't be a very expensive repair."

" I haven't finished with this matter," said the sergeant. " If I find . . ."

" Good morning, Sergeant," said Carolus cheerfully and left him.

Before leaving Brenstead he went to call on Elspeth.

" I've done all I can here," he said. " I'm afraid I've come to think your husband did swallow those tablets after all."

" Oh, Carolus, I don't know whether to be glad or sorry. I don't think I could have borne to go through it all again if you'd found it was someone else's doing, and yet I should have liked it known that he did not commit suicide."

" I shan't forget it altogether," said Carolus. " But there's no more I can do here. Perhaps something will come to light later. I'll give you my address and phone number. If anything happens you would like to tell me about I'll come over at once."

" That's nice of you. Will you be seeing Magnus?"

" I expect so."

" Tell him to come over. There are a lot of things I want to discuss with him."

" I will. I don't suppose I'll see him for a day or two, though."

" You have a house of your own in Newminster?"

" Yes. What's more my housekeeper's away at the moment. So I'm not looking forward to going back to it."

" Why not stay on in Brenstead till she gets back?"

" I can't. I've got a lot to do."

"But you said you'd finished with the whole case?"

" Not quite," said Carolus. " There is someone that you all seem to have forgotten. I want a little chat with him."

" Who's that?"

" The man in the railway compartment. The man who said that Felix would not be coming. Remember?"

" Yes. Of course. I've heard all about him. But mightn't it have been just a casual stranger?"

" It might. But I don't think it was."

" You don't mean you've traced him? You are clever."

" I haven't talked to him yet, but I know who he is and where to find him. I hope to see him in a day or two. I like tying up the loose ends. Well, good-bye, Elspeth."

" Good-bye, Carolus. I wish we could have met in happier circumstances."

She came to the front door to let him out. It was a fine spring morning and Carolus thought she looked almost beautiful as she stood there smiling.

Having the length of Manor Lane to cover, Carolus drove slowly, noticing once again the houses to left and right. It struck him that this piece of high suburbia had been the centre of his investigations. He liked it no more than he had done at first but he had proved to himself that even the dullest and most pretentious houses could be inhabited by people who in a case like this became interesting.

Approaching the Limpoles' villa, he saw that once again Edward Limpole was working in the garden, this time not at the trench he intended for a compost heap, but stooping over a bed near the gate. Carolus decided to stop.

" I'm leaving Brenstead," he said when he had greeted the stooping figure.

" You are?" A somewhat cunning smile spread over Edward's face. " I thought you'd come to find out all about the death of Felix Parador."

" I did, yes."

" And have you found out?" Edward seemed to be sharing some joke with the seedlings he was planting out.

" All I can for the moment," said Carolus.

Edward nodded slowly.

" It wasn't as easy as you thought, was it? You can't see through everybody as though they're glass."

" Are you taking another week off?"

" No. Just a couple of days. My brother thought I ought to stay with my sister for a time. She's going through one of her very bad times. Imagining things, you know."

" I'm very sorry. But you seem to be enjoying it."

" I have my garden."

" It's such a splendid day, too."

" I don't care for spring weather," said Edward. " Very treacherous."

" I'll come back some time," he told Edward before he walked away.

" I know you will. Good-bye," replied Edward stooping down again.

But before he got into his car he saw, not twenty yards away and walking up the other side of the lane, Chatty Dogman. She carried a fair-sized basket.

" Hullo, darling. Yes, do take the bloody thing. It's so mean

127

of Willy James to lock the car every day now. Just because I had that little tiny smash—well, it wasn't a smash really—with a woman in a Rolls. I mean a Rolls driven by a woman. At least she had a chauffeur. But you know what I mean."

" Of course."

" This is the house, darling. Oh, of course you remember it. You've been here, haven't you? That night when that frightful woman from somewhere told poor Elspeth that Felix had married her or something. I remember. You must come in and have a drink after lugging that all this way, darling. Oh, but you must."

"I really ought . . ."

" I've got a rather good new thing. Gin and bitter orange. Frightfully good, darling. It seems to work more quickly than other things, if you know what I mean."

Carolus followed her into the room of the party.

" Oh God!" she said, throwing off her fur coat. " I hope I haven't lost my diamond clasp. No, thank God, here it is. Willy James says I ought to keep my bits and pieces at the bank. I've got one or two rather good things, *all* from my side of the family, I might add. Willy James has hardly given me anything, really. Yes, he wants to put it in the bank for me. But darling I should never see it again. He'd have one of his bad times and need it to tide him over. I know him too well. Besides, there's no need to put it in a bank. Is that how you like it, darling?"

" Yes, thanks."

" No need at all. Willy James has a revolver."

Carolus stared a little blankly.

" No need to stare like a ghost, darling. A lot of bookies have revolvers. Everybody thinks they keep money in the house. It's nothing unusual. Only no one's supposed to know."

It was apparent that when Chatty raised her glass and said, " First today!" as she did now, she was using a figure of speech. She was not drunk but she could fairly be described as tiddly.

" Mind you," she said, swaying slightly, " I'm not altogether sorry you're going. I don't think you're doing anyone here much good. In fact I'm damn sure you're not. Look at that ghastly woman you brought to my party the other night. Shouting at Elspeth. I don't call that very good behaviour."

"I didn't bring . . ."

"Then upsetting people. All these enquiries you're making. People have got quite enough to worry about without that, darling. In fact I think it will be a damn good thing when you're gone if you ask me. Have another teeny one, darling?"

Carolus refused quite unruffled by her outburst.

"I know Willy James has enough to worry about anyway. Up late every night—God knows what he's doing. I don't know why you came here at all, but I do know you make things worse. However, cheers, darling. Happy days."

Carolus made his escape and this time succeeded in walking back to the car and driving off. There was one rather curious spectacle, though, before he reached The Royal Oak, that was Mrs. Boggett mounting her scooter and riding gamely away. He was reminded of a circus he had once seen in which a huge bear rode a miniature cycle round the ring.

Boggett himself was in the Oak.

"You heard about the will?" he asked Carolus with an air of mystery when he had drawn him aside. "Thriver's been telling them all what's coming to them and what's not. There's a nice little bit for me. More than I expected. Enough to Have a Few with. And there's One I've been noticing, lives near the station. Only wants taking out and a little money spending on her . . ."

"Who else has been told?"

"Here's the laugh. The poor bloody vicar's been cut out altogether. Done one of his jokes once too often. He won't laugh now. The boy still gets it but not till he's twenty-two."

"Does Mr. Hopelady know this?"

"Must do. I saw him this morning and you should have seen his face. White as a sheet, he was. Must be a big blow to him. The doctor's out, too, but I don't think he minds a— *She's* got money if he hasn't."

"What else do you know about Mr. Parador's will?"

"Isn't that enough? Only thing is when I told my old woman she said she was going to give up going out to work. So profits

129

on the roundabout are losses on the swings. I hear you're going away?"

"Yes. This afternoon."

"Found out all you wanted to know?"

"Pretty well for the moment, thanks."

"I could always ask the old woman if she's got anything else to tell you."

"Thank you, Boggett, but I think I've cleared up most of the points I wanted to know."

"You think he swallowed those sleeping tablets?"

"Yes. I do."

"I've said so all along. Stands to reason, doesn't it?"

"No," said Carolus firmly. "Tell me, what has happened to Gobler?"

"Old Gobler? I hear he's not so well. Not so well at all. That was more of a crack than anyone thought for at the time, it seems."

"I haven't seen him since the day the doctor took him home."

"No more has anyone else, as far as I can hear. What would happen if he was to peg out, I wonder? They'd have to find out who'd done it, wouldn't they?"

"I suppose so. If they could."

"I did hear they'd taken him into hospital. But you hear lots of things."

"I do," said Carolus, and went upstairs to pack.

But Carolus had one more encounter before he left Brenstead, and it was a very distressing one. He had paid his bill and was leaving when a boy whom he recognised as one of Hopelady's children approached him and said his father would like to see Carolus before he left. For a moment Carolus wondered whether this was yet another of the vicar's practical jokes, but remembering what Boggett had said, he told the boy to jump in and drove to the vicarage.

He found Mr. Hopelady very far from practical joking. He looked pale, as Boggett said, as though he had not slept all night. His fingers played nervously with his pipe and tobacco which he did not succeed in bringing to the point of lighting.

" I take it you know about Parador's will," he said and added rather bitterly, " You seem to know about everything."

" I do, yes," said Carolus. " I understand he has left your eldest son five thousand pounds."

" Yes. But this was left to me originally. Parador told me so. It was to be used to help in bringing up all the children."

" So I have heard. It does seem rather harsh."

" Over nothing. Nothing at all. A small practical joke. No sane man would have done such a thing. That's what I wanted to ask you, Deene. Do you think Parador *was* sane? I begin to doubt it. To make these sudden changes, then commit suicide. It cannot be called the conduct of a sane man."

" I'm afraid there is no evidence of anything else. You would have to prove that he was certifiably mad to have the will disproved. His lawyer was perfectly satisfied with the condition of his mind when he signed it. In fact I'll go farther and say that I don't think there was anything insane about his revenge on what you describe as a practical joke. You told me he had no sense of humour. This may have been *his* idea of a joke, Mr. Hopelady."

" You mean? If so, it's too cruel. Too cruel. I have my family. The money would have been a godsend. I could have sent Matthew to a public school instead of the Brenstead Tech."

" If you're so sure he'd have been better off, why don't you approach the executors? They may agree with you."

The vicar shook his head.

" There were so many things I could have done," he said, and Carolus saw to his embarrassment that he was near tears.

" Anyhow," he went on, recovering himself, " you don't think I would have any hope if I disputed the validity of the will? It seems so extraordinary, the way it has turned up weeks after Parador's death."

" Yes," agreed Carolus, rising to go. " That *is* extraordinary. Most extraordinary. But I don't see how it can in any way invalidate it. However, I'm not a lawyer."

He left, and this time there was no watering-can being emptied from above.

Chapter Thirteen

IT WAS PLEASANT TO REACH HIS HOME AND HAVE THE DOOR
opened by Mrs. Stick before he could get out his latch-key.

"I'm glad you're come, sir. I've got the young gentleman in
bed upstairs with a nasty chill and it's Ladies' Night at the Druids
tonight which would have meant me missing it."

Carolus seeking his way among these seemingly disconnected
remarks realised the sense of them.

"But it's not till eight o'clock so you've plenty of time if you
want to Have Something before I go or I can Leave It Out for
you."

Carolus hung up his coat.

"I should like a whisky and soda first," he said, and went
into his small library where a bright fire was burning.

"It's been a lovely day here. But I knew you'd like a bit of fire
when you came in," said Mrs. Stick when she brought the tray
and set it down by Carolus. "Yes, a nasty chill the young gentleman's got. It's going out on that motor-cycle's done it. I wonder
you allowed him to have it, sir, I really do. They're not safe,
those things. It's a miracle he hasn't broken his neck before now.

As it is his temperature's been up to over a hundred."

"How's Stick?"

"You know what Stick is. He'll want to know what you've found out about this gentleman he worked for."

"Tell him I've no information yet."

"Then there's Mr. Gorringer."

"Hasn't he left for Belgium?"

"By what I hear he won't be going this year. I don't know all about it but it seems something's gone wrong where he usually stays and he's decided to stop here so I expect he'll be round when he knows you're back. Which he will do because that Muggeridge was hanging about when you came in. Have you put the car away, sir? That means you're not going out tonight?"

"No. I'll keep an eye on Priggley."

"Then I'll tell Stick it'll be all right for us to go. Not that he'd miss it, anyway."

There was a ring at the front door.

"I shouldn't be surprised but what that was Mr. Gorringer," said Mrs. Stick, hurrying out.

Carolus heard the loud familiar voice in the hall and in a few moments the headmaster was with him.

"Ah, my dear Deene," he said. "I trust you will forgive this intrusion. I have just been informed of your return and as there were several little matters on which I wanted a word with you I took the liberty of calling."

"A drink, headmaster?"

"That would be most welcome. We have had our little troubles since I saw you, Deene. It will be the first time in many years that we have not spent our Easter vacation in Ostend."

"With days, of course, in Bruges," put in Carolus.

"With days, as you say, in the beautiful old city of Bruges. But our dear Madame Poinsteau, for many years the presiding genius of Pension Balmoral, has most unexpectedly decided to marry. Someone connected with the shipyards at Antwerp, I understand, a widower of considerable fortune. She decided to sell the Balmoral which is already in the hands of a couple from

133

Ghent whom I do not know. Madame Poinsteau acquainted us with the circumstances."

"I see. So you're staying here."

"Reluctantly, yes. My wife has taken it in very good part and made several clever witticisms about this matrimonial entanglement in the autumn of life. But I shall miss my annual change of scene. Now, Deene, to sterner matters. I understand that you have been in one of our new dormitory towns—Brenstead, I believe?"

"Yes."

"And that your visit has not been unconnected with the recent demise of one of its leading citizens? Just so. I also hear that a Coroner's Court has pronounced on the case but that you have seen fit to disagree with the verdict. Now all this would be no concern of mine, my dear Deene, were it not for one circumstance. Your life in the holidays is your own. But you had with you during your investigations a pupil from this school, a difficult pupil whom I myself had entrusted to your care. In a word, the boy Priggley."

"I didn't see much of him, as a matter of fact," said Carolus in that casual tone which Mr. Gorringer so disliked.

"It was my hope that you *would* see much of him. He is sorely in need of the steadying influence of an older man."

"He had the unsteadying influence of a younger woman. But that I understand is finished."

"I sincerely hope so. You have no plans to return to this town?"

"Not for the moment. Anyway, Priggley's laid up with a chill."

"I am naturally sorry to hear of his illness but I cannot resist the hope that it will keep him out of harm's way. Did you reach any conclusions in the case of this Mr. Parador?"

"It is not a pleasant case."

"You don't mean that it is in any way dangerous?"

"I don't know. It's the first time for some years I've found it necessary to carry a revolver."

The headmaster sat up with a jerk that was not dramatised.

" A revolver, Deene? Are you serious?"

Carolus pulled a .38 from his side pocket.

" But this is shocking. Please put that firearm out of sight. I feel it my duty to say . . ."

At that moment he was interrupted. Mrs. Stick, entering behind him, let out a scream and dropped a salver on which was a siphon of soda-water.

" Look at him!" she said shrilly, pointing to the window.

Carolus turned, but not fast enough. No face was to be seen.

" A face at the window, Mrs. Stick?" said Mr. Gorringer, rising to his feet.

" With goggles! I saw it as plain as a pike-staff. Looking in, he was. Oh my God!"

" This must be investigated," said Mr. Gorringer, making for the door.

"Don't open the front door!" shouted Carolus who was standing close to the window but almost wholly protected by the wall, watching the exterior. " Don't open the front door, you dam' fool!"

He was too late. Mr. Gorringer had pulled back the handle of the Yale lock and done exactly what Carolus had warned him against.

There was an eerie silence for about twelve seconds. Then, visible through the doorway of the room, Mr. Gorringer was seen moving slowly backwards, his hands above his head.

Carolus acted. Pulling out his .38 he fired once, blindly, at the window. The din in the small room was terrific and the window itself seemed to explode. Then a more welcome sound—someone was running towards the front gate. A car door slammed and a car, whose engine had been kept running, could be heard moving off rapidly.

The whole incident had occupied less than two minutes. Carolus calmly put his revolver back in his pocket.

" You'd better have a drink, Mrs. Stick," he said.

" I never touch it," said Mrs. Stick faintly. She was white and shivering. Carolus slopped out some whisky and poured it between her teeth. Then he turned to the headmaster and saw that he was also in a bad way. A peculiar patchiness appeared in his cheeks and his eyes were glazed and staring.

"I must sit down," he said, and did so.

Carolus took more time in serving him and did not need to pour it between his teeth.

Priggley and Stick appeared together.

"Go straight back to bed," Carolus told Priggley. "You've missed what little there was to see. They're miles away by now."

"*They*?" groaned Mr. Gorringer. "Were there several of them?"

"Someone else was driving. Your wife's all right, Stick. She's had a bit of a scare."

Mrs. Stick turned furiously on her husband.

"This is what comes of you starting things!" she said. "We're lucky to be alive, if you want to know. I never thought I'd come to be shot at. Oh, my God!"

Carolus made a sign to Priggley, who disappeared.

"Has she been shot at?" asked Stick.

"She has had a very unnerving experience, Stick," said Carolus. He had indeed seen Mrs. Stick angry before now, but never frightened, while Mr. Gorringer seemed to be in something like a stupor.

Carolus took a drink himself and waited for the inevitable questions and recriminations which would come when the two had recovered.

Mr. Gorringer was the first to speak.

"How do you know they will not return?" he asked, glancing uneasily at the window.

"They won't," said Carolus, "but Stick can close the shutters if you'll feel easier."

Stick began to do so.

"Do you realise," asked Mr. Gorringer in a hollow voice, "that I have been threatened with a revolver? That I stood for several moments with the barrel of a pistol almost touching my stomach?"

"I told you not to open the door."

"In very disrespectful terms, yes," agreed Mr. Gorringer. "I thought, in fact, you had taken leave of your senses when I heard you address me in that manner. And why not open the door? Are we to be menaced by people peering through our windows at night without trying to identify them? Or in your wisdom did you know who it was?"

"Yes. I knew."

"You knew! Perhaps you knew his reason for coming here?"

"Of course. He wanted to kill me."

Mrs. Stick gave a slight moan.

"To think it should come to this!" she said. "I've always known what this playing about with murder would mean sooner or later. I've told you a dozen times. Fancy shooting at anyone."

"I didn't shoot at anyone, Mrs. Stick."

"Then I'd like to know what that window's doing with a hole in it."

"I just shot into space."

"You can tell that to the police when they come for you in a minute. Someone's sure to have heard it and I'd like to know what you're going to say."

"I *have* got a licence for it," said Carolus mildly.

"Not for letting it off at people, you haven't. Suppose you was to have hit anyone."

"Did I understand you to say . . ." Mr. Gorringer was quite recovering his manner, "that this assailant of ours intended to kill you?"

"Of course. What else would have brought him here?"

"It seemed more probable at the time that he intended to kill me. It was at my stomach that his weapon pointed."

"You were in his way. That's why I let off that shot at the window. He had to clear out. Whoever was in the car might have gone without him. He has given up his attempt for tonight and tomorrow, he knows, will be too late. I don't think anyone can have noticed that shot. The bogey-wagon would have been here before now. If it was heard at all it was put down as a car back-firing. Shots so often are."

"You mean the police will not investigate this incident?" said Mr. Gorringer.

" They can't if they don't know about it, can they? Unless you want me to report it?"

" Far be it from me to bring to public notice anything so disgraceful. Can you not visualise the headlines in the more sensational newspapers? *Headmaster of The Queen's School, Newminster, in Shooting Affray. Famous Educationist Held at Pistol Point.* No, Deene, it is *not* my wish that you should report this. But it is my wish that you should realise once and for all where your reckless involvement in crime may land us. That a man in my public position, whose book of memoirs has brought him fame among modern headmasters, whose name has been carried by his pupils to the farthest corners of the earth, should be held at pistol point by a desperate criminal is monstrous, Deene, monstrous. And that this should happen in this quiet town of Newminster, at the house of one of his assistants, adds fuel to the flames."

" It's all over now, anyway," said Carolus soothingly.

" It may be for Some," said Mrs. Stick. " I shall never get over it to my dying day. Pistol shots all over the place—I'd only cleaned that window this morning and now look at it. If it hadn't been that Stick was partly to blame we'd have to pack up and go this very night. If you'd have seen that face at the window all covered up with goggles and that, you'd have said the same."

" You haven't yet told us why this man wanted to injure you," Mr. Gorringer pointed out to Carolus.

" He didn't want to injure me. That's the very last thing he wanted to do. He wanted to kill me."

" But why?" asked Mr. Gorringer who looked as though he shared some of the man's ambition.

" Because I know too much. It's not a novel motive. He is desperate. You are quite right there."

" If that is so," said Mr. Gorringer grimly, " I do not see that we have any guarantee against his return."

" Nor don't I," said Mrs. Stick. " We shall all be murdered in our beds. I've said so from the start. Once they get an idea like that in their heads, what's to stop them? That's what I'd like to know."

138

" If this man is a practiced criminal, as you say . . ."

" I didn't say practiced. I said desperate. If he were a practiced criminal he wouldn't have messed it up that time. He could have shot me through the window."

" There you go," said Mrs. Stick. " I shan't get a wink of sleep tonight. I don't know how you can stand there talking about shooting through the window as though it was a thing that happens to respectable people every day. I don't really."

" I've made no study of ballistics," admitted Mr. Gorringer, " but have I not read that a pane of glass may deflect the most accurate aim? To shoot a man with a pistol at a range of four yards, as you must have been to him, is no easy task, I opine, and he doubtless decided to make sure of his accuracy."

" No, it wasn't that," said Carolus, " but fortunately we were sitting by firelight. He could not distinguish me."

" And to think he was coming in at that very front door to do it!" said Mrs. Stick. " It's a wonder there's any of us left to tell the tale."

" I suppose that the sound of the shot you fired caused him to lose his nerve?" suggested Mr. Gorringer. " Or was he thinking of his confederate in the waiting car?"

" That's more like it," said Carolus. Then deciding that this inquest had gone on long enough, he said, " Mrs. Stick, you had better go and get ready for the Druids' Ladies' Night."

" I don't know what to do, I'm sure. I shan't enjoy a moment of it, thinking about what might have happened. Then there's your dinner to think of and the young gentleman. Stick will be heart-broke if I don't go and I promised Mrs. Spiner, but how do I know I shan't come back to find the house burnt to the ground?"

" I've told you they won't be back tonight. Now for goodness' sake stop frightening yourself and get ready. Headmaster, we must have another drink to celebrate our escape."

Mr. Gorringer was coming round to an appreciation of his own conduct.

" You're of the opinion, then, Deene, that if I had been forced to take one step farther back and our attacker had reached this

139

door, he would have shot you down in cold blood?"

"If I hadn't got him first, yes."

"In that case you must surely be warned against this foolhardy behaviour of yours in involving yourself in crime? Homicide has no place in our quiet educational backwater, and you must, after the events of tonight, begin to realise that. With one of your pupils sick upstairs, with your headmaster enjoying a moment's respite from domestic cares in your hospitable home, we have the murderous intrusion of a killer. Does it not make you consider?"

"I'm sorry it happened here," admitted Carolus.

"You were not anticipating events such as these?"

"I thought there might be some move. I never imagined this. But you're right, headmaster. I must take precautions. I'll send the Sticks away for a few days. Mrs. Stick is anxious to visit her sister in Battersea. I myself shall go to a place called Buttsfield."

"And Priggley?" questioned Mr. Gorringer anxiously.

"I thought perhaps you might care to take . . ."

"I am astounded that you should voice such a suggestion. As you know perfectly well, Mrs. Gorringer, in spite of a cheerful front, is by no means strong and I am in urgent need of a relief from all anxieties. Your proposition is quite unthinkable."

"Then he must go to Battersea," said Carolus. "Mrs. Stick's brother-in-law is a respectable undertaker and may be able to tame Priggley's exuberance better than you or I. Mrs. Stick has a quite unaccountable weakness for the little horror and will be glad to take him."

"There seems no other way," admitted the headmaster. "He certainly can't stay here. But what of the future? Are we to start next term under the menace of gunmen? Am I to expect my classes to be interrupted by incursions such as this evening's?"

"No, headmaster. I am not going to Buttsfield for nothing. It is the twin dormitory town to Brenstead and about twenty miles away. I think I can assure you that within a week this wretched business will be finished, one way or another."

"One way or another, Deene? I find something ominous in the words."

"Yes. It's tricky. I don't deny it's tricky. But it has got to be

140

wound up. We can't as you say, have our quiet educational back-water threatened in this way."

" Ah, Deene, incurably frivolous as ever. But I confess myself out of my depth here You must follow the guidance of your own conscience."

" That's just what I'm proposing to do," said Carolus as Mr. Gorringer rose to go.

Next morning, after a quiet night, Mrs. Stick vaccilated but finally agreed to the proposal.

" I won't deny I'd like to go to stay with my sister for a few days and Stick has quite a liking for Battersea Park. The young gentleman's normal this morning . . ."

" I beg your pardon, Mrs. Stick?"

" I mean his temperature's down. I don't see why he shouldn't travel with us. Of course he couldn't bring that motor-cycle of his—my sister would have a fit if she was to set eyes on it, but he said it had to go in to the garage anyway. We certainly can't stay here till that murderer's been caught. I shall have to ring up and ask if it's convenient, of course, but my sister's a great one for arranging things so I expect it will be all right."

It was.

" Only you must let me know as soon as it's safe to come back here, sir, and don't let my sister think there's been any trouble because she can't bear anything that Calls Attention. It doesn't do, with her husband being in the line he is."

Priggley agreed to lend Carolus his motor-cycle for some days. He seemed enchanted with the idea of Battersea.

Chapter Fourteen

WHEN HE HAD DRIVEN THE STICKS AND RUPERT TO THE STATION Carolus arranged that his garage should send a driver with the Bentley to Buttsfield and put it in a garage there in Carolus's name. He then made the journey on Priggley's Criterion motor-cycle.

He found Rosehurst, Brenstead Road, to be a villa rather of the type he had known in Brenstead itself except that it had a discreet sign reading *Residential Hotel*. He left his motor-cycle outside the gate and walked up to the front door hindered by the oilskin overalls he had purchased.

A harrassed-looking young woman opened the door.

" Rooms? I don't know whether we have or not. You better see my aunt about that. She'll be down in a minute."

As he approached this last episode in the matter of Felix Parador's death, an episode which he knew would be grim, sordid and dangerous, Carolus thought how commonplace was this setting with a faint smell of cooking in the air and ugly Victorian furniture about him. He had not even known that such residential hotels existed and certainly had not expected to find one in the dormitory town of Buttsfield, yet it was Rosehurst that seemed normal, complacent, sure of itself, and the new town of Buttsfield that was outré. And when Mrs. Hamley appeared the impression was confirmed, for she was a stout, comfortable-looking party with a very pink face and bright grey hair, just what one might have expected the proprietress of a residential hotel to be.

"Come in," she said looking anxiously at his overalls, "unless you'd like to take those off first? I know my nephew always does. The gentlemen's cloakroom is there."

Feeling distinctly more at ease, Carolus faced Mrs. Hamley across a bearskin hearthrug.

"I understand you wanted a room," she said. "Would it be for some time?"

"Some weeks, yes," said Carolus. "I'm with an insurance company, you see."

Mrs. Hamley picked up her knitting.

"You would be alone?"

"Oh, yes. Quite."

"It happens that we have a single room. But it's not very large and at the top of the house. There are two rooms up there and the other is occupied by my nephew."

"I don't mind a small room," said Carolus.

"It's quite a comfortable little room and my nephew is a very quiet young man, except when he's on his motor-cycle."

"I'm a motor-cyclist myself."

"Then you'll get on with George. He's mad on the thing. Here, there and everywhere. For his business, of course. He's with an estate agent here. But I believe he's thinking of leaving. He tells me he has made a successful speculation on his own account. He's always been ambitious."

"What is the charge for the room you have free?"

"We don't do lunches," explained Mrs. Hamley. "You get a good English breakfast and a meal at night. I have to charge ten guineas, I'm afraid."

Carolus agreed to this and paid a week in advance as his luggage, he said was being brought by a friend later in the day.

His room was an attic with a small electric fire with a coin-insertion meter. The bed was narrow and the carpet sparse. This was the kind of living which must make bachelordom impossible, he thought.

But at last he had run to earth the most mysterious figure in this curious affair, the man in the train, the face at the window, and found him to be—on paper at least—George Catford, nephew to the cosy Mrs. Hamley, employee in an estate agent's, keen motor-cyclist, an everyday member of the community.

Yet his first sight of George Catford that evening in the ill-lit hall was somehow both eerie and forbidding. Catford had just come in, having ridden up on his motor-cycle, and was garbed in black oilskins. He stood quite motionless as Carolus approached, watching intently, and for a sickening moment Carolus thought he must have identified him somehow. When Catford spoke it was in that curiously deep voice which had so impressed the men in the railway compartment, and also Flood.

"Is that your motor-cycle outside?" he asked.

"Yes."

"Same as mine. Criterion. You staying here?"

"For a time," said Carolus, not too cordially.

"What brings you to Buttsfield?" asked George Catford, remaining immobile. There was something feline in his steady observant stare.

"Business," retorted Carolus.

It was his policy from the first to make all the advances come from Catford.

"Cagey, aren't you? I'm only asking."

"I know. It's all right. I've got a lot on my mind," said Carolus.

George Catford at last moved towards the little cloakroom in which Carolus had removed his overalls.

That was their first unpromising encounter and it left Carolus with an unpleasant taste in his mouth. There was something which Mrs. Stick would have called 'creepy' about George Catford. But he knew that the young man was curious about him.

There was a communal dining-room in which were a number of small tables rather close together, and when Carolus came down he found his place had been laid at Catford's.

"If you'd rather sit at the big table you can," Catford said. "But you'll be asked all your business there."

"All right. Thanks," said Carolus, taking his place.

"This is my aunt's hotel. She thinks everyone ought to mix. It's not my idea."

"Nor mine," said Carolus.

"Haven't I seen you before somewhere?"

"I shouldn't think so. I only arrived today. Got some insurance work to do in the district."

"Ah. I'm with Willows and Willows the estate agents. But I don't expect to be here much longer. I want to go abroad. Had enough of this place."

"Where d'you mean to go?"

"Don't know yet. Away from all this. I've always had a fancy for Algeria."

"Disturbing at present, I should have thought."

"I should like that. I'm not a home-loving type."

Then the conversation became technical.

"What can you get out of that bike of yours?" asked Catford, and Carolus who had as usual mugged up his facts was able to reply. He saw Mrs. Hamley beaming across the room.

Catford said nothing which might not have been said by any young estate agent in a place like Rosehurst, yet Carolus knew that he was not mistaken in thinking that about him there was something very odd indeed, something sinister and quite ruthless. Trying to analyse his feelings about Catford, Carolus came to the conclusion that in a sense he was not real, was not in the least what he appeared to be and only spoke from the upper crust of his mind while underneath, his manner, out of sight and hearing of those who knew him, was another self, primitive, cruel and greedy for power. The man was a potential murderer. People were nothing to him; in his jungle dreams he dominated the world. But all this came with time. On that first evening Carolus only knew that he had not come to Rosehurst in vain.

145

Like so many schizophrenics, however, Catford could not keep his mouth shut. He was under an impulse stronger than himself to impress Carolus. Perhaps he had been starved of love as a child, perhaps he had been born with a tormenting subconscious knowledge of his own mediocrity which made him cry for someone's admiration, or perhaps he recognised in Carolus all he could never be. Whatever the cause, as the days passed he grew more and more arrogant and boastful and more revealing of his inner nature. Carolus listened fascinated to all he said and sometimes heard the voice of madness in it. Carolus allowed himself to be drawn into Catford's confidence as though unwillingly, but when he showed diffidence Catford grew more emphatic and far-fetched.

On the third night they had a drink together at the local.

" Though I don't drink much. Until lately I've concentrated everything on saving enough money to get out of England. I've been treated very unfairly in this country. Some day I may tell you all about it. I had to have the motor-bike, though. To get out of this town. I like to sit on a hill somewhere with a lot of the countryside spread out beneath me and think my own thoughts."

So did Hitler, reflected Carolus. But he encouraged him to go on.

" I've always had big ideas. Ever since I was a kid. I've always meant to be someone. I didn't mean to go on all my life working for others. I was determined to get to the top—quick."

" Big ideas, as you call them, may take a man to the top. Or they may land him in prison."

Catford fixed those cold eyes on him and said, " Someone been talking about me?"

" No. Why?"

" Because I have been in prison. Only six months on a faked-up charge about some cheques. So you may be right. One way or the other. But now it's going to be the other. I'm going right Up."

There was a long pause.

"D'you know the Great Ring, near here?" Catford asked suddenly.

Carolus stared at his glass, amazed at the question and wondering what was to come.

"Heard of it," he said.

"That's a place I like," he said. "I spend hours up there. I kind of feel at home. In the summer you can see four counties. You can't understand what I feel when I'm up there. Even at night I know it's all around me . . ."

The lunatic, the lover and the poet, thought Carolus. But George Catford was not mad in any ordinary sense of the word. There was no warmth in him. He confided in Carolus because it pleased him but he had not a thought for Carolus. Beyond his first cautious curiosity he had no interest in him at all.

"I've always believed my chance would come," he went on relentlessly. "I don't mean just come without my doing anything to find it. I don't believe in that. You've got to be ready for your chance."

"Chance of what?"

"Chance of getting on top. Chance of escaping a bloody life like I've had. Look at all the poor fools filling in the football pools and thinking it will come that way. Sitting there waiting for the results and saying 'someone's going to have it so it might be me!' I'm sorry for them. The chances are so big against them that it's the same as if they didn't buy a ticket. But if you watch, if you're ready to grab it, it will come all right. You can be sure of that. It has done for me."

"Have another drink?" said Carolus hopefully.

"No, thanks. I don't drink really. Don't need to. I can take things as they are. Don't need drink. A man like me . . ."

Carolus had been waiting for those words. 'A man like me' —what he meant was that there was no man like him. That he was unique.

"A man like me knows where he's going," went on George Catford. "Always have known. When I was at school I used to look at the other kids, and think you poor little sods, you're going to spend your whole lives working to feed yourselves, your wives and your children. All right, you can throw in television and a drink now'n again. But what else *are* they doing? Think I was going to be satisfied with that?"

Carolus lit a cheroot and watched him.

"How far have you got?" he asked gently, as though afraid to interrupt the man's thoughts.

Catford replied with a horrifying kind of inner exaltation. "How far have I got? I'm *there*."

"Rich?" ventured Carolus.

"Rich enough to get rich."

"I see. Yes, they say the first thousand's the hardest."

"They used to say that. Now it's the first five thousand. You've travelled a lot. Where would you go, if you were me? Money sticks to money. Only I want the right place. Africa? South America?"

"I don't know. I've no experience of . . . investment."

"I don't want to invest. I want to speculate. Watch it grow like that beanstalk in the story. It'll do that for me. I've always known it would once I could start it off. You see, my aunt brought me up. Both parents died before I knew them. One bomb got them both. My aunt's never understood the first thing about me. How could she? How could anyone? A man like me is never understood. But he's felt. There'll be a lot of people know about me."

Carolus tried to send him in a new direction.

"Do you ever think of getting married?" he asked.

For the first time Carolus saw George Catford's smile and it was not pleasant.

"Me? Married? Can you imagine it? I could never be tied down like that. If there was polygamy that might be different. I'd never stand married life as you understand it. When I'm right where I mean to be it will be time to think about women. I could have had plenty, mind you. There's one over at Brenstead now . . ."

"Brenstead! Do you know Brenstead?" asked Carolus innocently.

"Yes. Why?"

148

" It's only that I've got to go on there when I finish here. What's it like?"

" Much the same. I don't know it well. I know a man there called Scotter. A chemist. He was at school with me. But that's about all."

" Scotter," repeated Carolus. " Seem to know that name."

" I daresay. It's not uncommon." Catford obviously wanted to get back to his egomaniac monologue.

" When do you expect to leave Buttsfield?" Carolus asked.

" Very soon now. There's just one more formality to go through. It might be tomorrow or the next day. It won't be much longer. *I'll* see to that. Then you won't see me for dust. Pity you can't tell me where to go, though."

To hell, thought Carolus, to roast along with all the other Nazi-minded swine. For this was the fascist mentality par excellence. What a gauleiter George Catford would have made. What a chief for a death camp. Yet, like all megalomaniacs he had something pitiful about him.

They went back to Rosehurst and before going up to bed Catford opened the door of his aunt's little sitting-room.

" Been a phone call for me this evening?"

" No, George."

So that was how it was to come, thought Carolus. His big chance. A phone call. But Carolus locked the door of his room that night.

In the morning he went to make certain preparations for eventualities which he now saw as inevitable. A couple of hundred yards away was a vast municipal car park, for the planners of Buttsfield had shown remarkable foresight when they laid out the town in realising that private motor cars would increase to unheard of numbers in the next few years. Remembering Mr. Flood, he expected to find an attendant with a keen eye to the main chance and was pleasantly impressed with Joe Coke, a merry old character in a peaked cap.

" Is there anything against a car being here all night?" he asked.

Mr. Coke at once put himself on the side of the revolting

149

angels by talking of 'They', the almighty, the unidentifiable to whom most of us refer with distaste several times a day.

"They don't like it," he said, "and sometimes The Law come round taking numbers. But I've no objection."

Carolus passed a handsome tip.

"It's like this," he said. "I've got a Bentley at Thompsett's Garage and I want to bring it here. I'm staying at Rosehurst and this would be handy."

"You're going to lock it up, I hope?"

"Yes. For what that's worth. The point is that I may want it in a hurry."

"There's no reason why you shouldn't have it in a hurry. We'll pop it in somewhere where no one can get in your way getting out. How would that be?"

"Admirable. It may stay there one night or perhaps more. I can't be certain about that."

"That'll be all right, sir. You bring it along. I'll keep an eye on it in the mornings. I'm off in the afternoons but I come on again at seven till after the Pictures come out. You don't need to worry about it in those times, but I can't answer for the night. You'll have to take the chance of anyone driving off in it then."

"I understand that. Where would you propose to put it?"

"What about over in that corner? Backed in, so you could get out at once if you wanted to. That car you see has been left here for a month and they're deciding what to do with it, so you won't have to worry about that. I'll see nothing gets stood in front of it."

"Very well. I'll bring it round now."

So far as he could tell, Carolus was unobserved as he brought the car and backed it into the place indicated.

"There we are," said Mr. Coke, beaming with satisfaction. "Just right, isn't it? Handy for you to slip out any minute you want."

Carolus returned to Rosehurst and about six o'clock that evening found an excuse to go into Mrs. Hamley's little sitting-room. She invited him to sit down and did exactly what he hoped and expected her to do—talked about George Catford.

150

" I was so pleased to see you two getting on so well. I expect it's those motor-cycles of yours. George never takes much interest in the people we have staying here. But then he's always been one on his own, as you might say, even when he was a little chap. I used to think that was through him losing his mother and father when he was small but now I don't know. I think he'd have been the same if they'd have lived. It's his character.

" He was always a bit of a handful and it made it difficult for me because my husband never really took to him. We hadn't a boy of our own and my daughter—that's her photo there on the bureau—didn't get on with him too well either. But I felt it my duty after my sister was killed and I must say he's had everything a son of mine would have had."

Except love, Carolus thought, rather bleakly.

" I won't say he didn't appreciate it. I suppose he may have in his way, but you could never tell what he was thinking. I tried to believe he was a good boy at heart and stuck up for him with my husband, but many's the night I've not slept for worrying about him. ' George '. I used to say, ' you want the earth. Why aren't you satisfied with what other people have?' But no. It was always something. Then about three years ago—I don't know whether I ought to tell you—he Got into Trouble. You can imagine how it upset us, in the papers and everything, and my husband said he'd never have him in the house again, which you can't blame him for really.

" When my husband died last year, I had to send for him. I couldn't bear to think of him not being at the funeral. At first he wouldn't go at all. Then he said he Wouldn't Wear Black, until I got him a suit and tie and socks and everything which he said was a waste of money. But he wore it all the same and came to the funeral with the rest of us."

" Did he ever wear his mourning clothes again?"

" It's funny you should ask that. I was surprised myself. It was a couple of weeks or so ago. He came in very late as he often does and went out early morning. When I went to his room I found he'd put on his Black. He didn't go to the office that day and came in before tea-time. ' George!', I said, ' whatever are you wearing your Black for?' ' Been to a funeral ', he said but he wouldn't tell me any more about it. You see what he is?"

Carolus nodded.

" After his uncle died he behaved very quiet for a few days and I hadn't the heart to let him go anywhere else to live when we had one of the top rooms empty. So he's been here ever since. He got that job with Willows and Willows but I'm afraid he won't keep it. He talks of going abroad and I suppose that might be the best thing for him."

She was interrupted by the sound of the front door.

" They start coming in now," she said. " I must go and see about the evening meal."

Chapter Fifteen

THAT WAS THE FIRST TIME MRS. HAMLEY CONFIDED IN CAROLUS about George but it seemed to set a precedent and on the following day she continued as though confident that Carolus shared her anxieties about him. This gave Carolus a sense of rising tension, for George himself had grown taciturn and Carolus knew that he, too, was approaching what he called 'his big chance' but for which Carolus would have used another name.

"He went up to London yesterday," said Mrs. Hamley in little more than a whisper. "Goodness knows what for. I wish I knew what he was up to. It worries me. I suppose he doesn't say anything to you?"

"He didn't tell me he was going."

"No. There you are. He's got something on his mind. I oughtn't to say it, Mr. Deene, but there are times when I wonder if he's quite Right. He'd stop at nothing, I truly believe, if it stood in his way."

That evening George looked into his aunt's sitting-room on his way upstairs and not seeing Carolus asked if there had been a phone call for him.

" Not while I've been here," said Mrs. Hamley.

" That's another thing," she confided when Catford had gone. " He's waiting for a phone call from someone."

" A girl, perhaps?"

" No, it's a man's voice. It's come through once or twice and he won't give his name. There was one rather late on the night before you arrived, as a matter of fact. What do you make of that?"

" Could be anything, couldn't it?"

" But there's something I don't like about it, Mr. Deene."

There was something Carolus did not like about it, did not like at all. But he said nothing more.

That evening when he faced George Catford across the table in the dining-room he found him moody and silent.

" You coming round to the local this evening?" asked Carolus cheerfully.

" I don't know. I'm waiting for a call."

At nine o'clock it came. Both Carolus and George Catford were in their respective rooms, both in a sense waiting for it. There was only one private telephone at Rosehurst, in Mrs. Hamley's room, and a money-in-the-slot telephone in the hall. This was evidently on Mrs. Hamley's for she came to the foot of the attic stairs and called, " George! you're wanted on the phone. That man who won't give his name again."

It flashed across the mind of Carolus that murderous crime was made more macabre by its association with the common-place, that good, comfy Mrs. Hamley calling her nephew to receive an ominous call, speaking in her housewifely way as any aunt might speak to any nephew, made the situation infinitely more grim than if it had been announced by some hooded gangster. He waited until Catford had hurried downstairs then prepared quietly to follow him.

But after a few minutes he heard Catford coming upstairs again and dived quickly back into his room. Catford went into his own room and locked the door. Listening intently, Carolus heard movements and something was dragged across the floor. Probably Catford was packing.

154

Carolus waited. If his mind had been less alertly concentrated on the matter in hand he might have smiled to find himself sitting on an uncomfortable chair in a musty boarding house waiting for a monomaniac young man to prepare himself for an escape. He believed with Mrs. Hamley that Catford would stop at nothing that stood in his way and Carolus knew that he was the only man living who could prevent the denouement ahead. Could and must prevent it at whatever cost for it meant nothing less than saving a life. But he could do nothing unless Catford left the house, unless that phone call had represented his ' great chance ', unless he was going to an appointment.

So he sat there until he heard Catford's door quietly opened and the key turned from the outside. When Catford started slowly descending and had reached the landing of the first floor, Carolus opened his own door as silently. The lower staircase was carpeted so he could only guess that Catford had reached the hall, until he heard the door of the cloakroom open and shut. So he was putting on his overalls. At last he came out and this time there was no mistaking the sound of the front door which could not be closed from outside without a slight slamming noise.

Carolus still moved without unnecessary speed. He went down to the hall and listened for the sound of Catford's motor-cycle. Yes, he had started it up and gone out of the gate.

Now Carolus hurried. He was aware of Mrs. Hamley coming into the hall and asking some anxious question—' Where has he gone?' or something of the sort. He left the house and covered the two hundred yards to the car park in time that would not have disgraced an athlete.

Then he saw what he had subconsciously feared—someone had backed a car in front of his, its tail lights within a foot or two of his bumper.

Mr. Coke came across.

" Now I wonder how he managed to slip in there," he said amiably. " Must have been when I wasn't noticing."

Carolus, who had tried the doors of the small car and found them locked, did not hesitate for a moment but from the boot of his own car he pulled out a heavy jack and smashed the window of the driver's seat..

"You can't do that," said Mr. Coke, too late for truth. "You'll get me into trouble. Look what you've done!"

Carolus was already leaning through to open the door of the car and release the hand-brake.

"What's he going to say when he comes back?" demanded Mr. Coke, who, in spite of himself, was helping to push the car forward.

"Tell him I'll pay for the damage," said Carolus unlocking the door of the Bentley. "Deene. Rosehurst."

Mr. Coke was still gaping in wonder as Carolus drove out of the parking place and took the road towards Brenstead. There was only one set of lights to cross and he saw they were green.

But he realised that he might be too late.

It was a fast road, but it had been a fast road for George Catford, he reflected, and there was little chance of overtaking him except through an accident or breakdown.

As he approached the Great Ring Carolus slowed down. The car park was not visible from the road but the narrower way which connected it with the road, two or three hundred yards of tarmac for those who wanted to visit the ancient monument, could be seen from some distance in daylight. Tonight as Carolus approached there was no sign of a light from this road but as he watched, the headlights of a car became visible. Someone was driving down the gentle hill.

Carolus stopped and turned off his headlights. Then as the car was cautiously coming out on the main road ahead of him he switched them on and identified the car at once. It was Mr. Hopelady's old Triumph and it gathered speed on the road ahead, making towards Brenstead.

Carolus did not follow. There was no point in overtaking the car at this point. He turned towards the Great Ring and came up to the car park.

His headlights showed him in the far corner of the area something which kept him moving in that direction. He stopped, and leaving his headlights on, walked across. Lying beside his motor-

156

cycle which was on its side on the ground was George Catford. He was dead and it did not take Carolus long to find the cause. He had been shot in the back of the head.

Carolus stood looking down on the man and cycle for several moments. If it was a revolver bullet which had passed through the cranium, entering rather low in the back of the skull and emerging through the forehead, it had been fired at close range, for there were few who could aim a pistol with such accuracy from any distance. While merely guessing about something which experts would be able to decide easily enough, he supposed that Catford had ridden up, seen someone whom he expected to see waiting for him, dismounted and was engaged in pulling his cycle up on to its stand when he was shot from close behind.

Petrol was running from the motor-cycle but its lights had been switched off, perhaps by Catford himself. The young man lay on his side in an attitude that appeared almost restful. His big chance had ended in this.

Carolus made no detailed examination. It was not his way to interfere with what could more efficiently be done by the police who were experienced and competent in such things. He made a casual search for the weapon but found nothing. He left the corpse and cycle exactly as he had found them, turned the Bentley and drove down the slope to the main road, taking the Brenstead direction. He did not delay but he was not unduly hurried.

Arrived in Brenstead he made first for Manor Lane. There was a light in Boggett's cottage, he noticed, but other houses were in complete darkness, which considering it was not yet eleven o'clock seemed unusual even for a dormitory town. He pulled up short of the vicarage and saw the Triumph standing at the gate as it usually stood. The radiator was warm. He rang the bell.

There was a long delay, then Willa Hopelady came to the door, fully dressed.

" Oh, it's you. Whatever . . ."

" Could I see Mr. Hopelady, please? It's urgent."

" No. You could *not* see Mr. Hopelady," she said with spirit. " He's seriously ill and the doctor says no one is to disturb him."

" I'm sorry to hear that," said Carolus. " Did you know his car had been out this evening?"

" His *car*?" said Willa Hopelady in great surprise.

" Yes. It can't have been back long. The radiator is still warm."

" Then someone else must have taken it. My husband has been in bed since four o'clock yesterday when I found he had a temperature of 102°. The doctor was with him this evening."

" Sporlott?"

" Of course, Dr. Sporlott. It's very worrying because he's no better this evening. It's all the worry, I think, though Dr. Sporlott thinks it's flu."

" No one heard the car taken away?"

" I don't know who you are or what you want but I'm not going to stand here answering questions all night. I've got my husband to look after. Of course no one heard the car driven away. I should have phoned the police if I'd known."

" I'm terribly sorry to trouble you, Mrs. Hopelady. But this is rather a serious matter. A man has been killed."

She showed no surprise.

" Then it's for the police to make enquiries," she said. " The number of road accidents . . ."

" This wasn't a road accident. Would you mind telling me what time the doctor was with your husband?"

" Wasn't a road accident? You don't mean . . .?"

" Yes. I do. And your husband's car was seen coming away from the place where it happened. That is why I asked you at what time the doctor was with him?"

" Eight or eight-thirty. Not later. Anyone could have taken his car. He never locks it. But he's not left his bed."

" And you have been with him?"

" All the time, of course. Now I must really . . ."

" Yes. Once again I'm sorry to have disturbed you. I hope the vicar will soon recover."

Willa Hopelady made no reply but firmly closed the front door.

There was nothing for it now but to go to the police station.

158

Carolus could only hope that someone more intelligent than Sergeant Beckett would be in charge.

But he was disappointed.

"So it's you again," said the sergeant as soon as Carolus walked in. "What is it this time? Your car has been scraped again? I know all about you, Mr. Deene; you're a schoolmaster who's been a nuisance to the police with your larking about with crime. But you're not going to be a nuisance to me again. You deliberately gave me false information last time you were here and it's not decided yet what steps we shall take about it. What have you come to report this time?"

"Murder," said Carolus quietly.

"What do you mean, murder?" shouted Sergeant Beckett. "You'll find yourself in serious trouble, you know. A police station is not a place to try that sort of game in."

"Can I see someone in the plain clothes branch?"

"That's for me to decide. You've led us up the garden once. I don't know whether you've been drinking or not, but you can't come in here talking about murder. We've got work to do."

"You certainly have. Now listen to me. A man was shot in the back of the head tonight . . ."

"All right. All right. Have it your own way. Only I warn you, Mr. Deene, if this is more of your foolery it will be a serious matter. What is it you wish to bring to my notice?"

"I've told you. A dead man—with a bullet through his head."

"Did you make the discovery or were you told about this?"

"Oh, for God's sake!"

"There's no need for blasphemy, Mr. Deene. Will you please make a detailed report in proper terms."

Carolus sighed.

"I was proceeding along the road from Buttsfield to Brenstead at approximately 9.50 this evening . . ."

"By car?"

"By car. As I approached the side-turning which leads to the Great Ring . . ."

"The Great Ring," said Sergeant Beckett who was scribbling busily.

" I noticed the headlights of a car approaching the road from the direction of the Great Ring."

" Speed?"

" Slowish. It turned into the main road and proceeded towards Brenstead. I turned at the junction and proceeded towards the car park of the Great Ring."

" Why did you do that?"

" Why not? As I reached the car park I saw the figure of a man prone on the ground beside an overturned motor-cycle from which the petrol was running."

" Registration number?"

" BYY 018."

Sergeant Beckett referred to some papers.

" That's the number you gave us before! In that other story of yours. Now I'm warning you for the last time, Mr. Deene . . ."

" I saw a Criterion motor-cycle, registration number BYY 018, lying on its side with petrol running from it. A dead man was beside it."

" How did you know he was dead?"

" He had a bullet hole through his head. From the back of the skull. I then proceeded to come here to report the matter."

" Are you subject to illusions of any kind? Any mental trouble in your family?"

" Lots," said Carolus, " but there is my report and you'd better get moving on it. You can't leave the man there all night."

" I will ask you to sign this," said the sergeant. " Thank you. Now this matter will be investigated. If it should prove that you have again been attempting to mislead us, proceedings will be taken against you. If there should happen to be anything in your report you will be required for further questioning. You are returning to Newminster where I understand you own some property?"

" I have a house. Yes, I shall be returning to Newminster tonight."

" Then in either case you will be hearing from us. You've no idea of the identity of the dead man, of course?"

" Oh yes. His name is George Catford."

" You are aware that that is the owner of the motor-cycle you gave the number of, and said it had scraped your car?"

" Yes. He was the owner."

" I see," said Sergeant Beckett, considering deeply. " There's something I don't understand about this. The same things keeping turning up in some way."

" Here's my address and telephone number in Newminster. I should be glad to see the detective-inspector who investigates the murder. I think I may be useful to him."

" If there has been an . . . accident of any serious kind you will be asked in due course to account for your movements. For the moment you may go."

Carolus decided that before he started on the long drive to Newminster he would go to the Old Manor House and see if Elspeth was still up. He badly wanted a drink.

He found lights on.

" Oh, Carolus, it's you. I was just going to bed. I've got some news for you."

Carolus took off his overcoat and noticed Rumble's hanging there. He joined Elspeth by a good bright fire.

" You won't be the first to hear it because it was settled last night."

" You're going to be married?"

" That's it. Jimmy wanted not to tell anyone because he thinks it's too soon after Felix's death but I tell him that's hopeless."

" Where is he?" asked Carolus. " I'd like to congratulate him."

" He's staying in this evening for an early night."

Carolus remembered the overcoat but thought it would not be tactful to press the point.

" Anyway, you must drink to us," said Elspeth. " What will you have?"

Carolus sat by the blazing fire and gave his congratulations.

" What brought you back to Brenstead?" Elspeth asked. " You're not still worrying about the other thing?"

" No. I've finished with that."

161

" I'm glad, now. I want to get away from here with Jimmy and perhaps live abroad. After all that's happened I don't want to keep this place on. It was always more Felix's home than mine. And the people are really rather awful."

" Some of them."

" Most, I think. They seem to think I'm responsible for Felix's will and I knew nothing about it. Hopelady's nearly off his head I'm told."

" He's not a very stable character, anyway. Where do you think you will go?"

" Spain, probably. I've persuaded Jimmy to sell his share in the travel agency. There's no point in our staying in England."

" I see your point. Personally, I'm never tempted to live abroad."

" By the way, you were going to find the man in the railway carriage. Did you succeed?"

" Yes. At least I found the man I think it was. I couldn't get him to say anything about it, though. He won't bother anyone any more now. You can be sure of that."

Elspeth smiled.

" He never bothered me," she said. " It was you who were so curious about him."

" I hate loose ends when I try to get at the truth. But I could learn nothing from him. And now he's dead."

" Dead?"

Elspeth was appalled at Carolus's cool announcement.

" Yes."

" How do you know?"

" Everyone will know tomorrow. But don't let it worry you. He wasn't a very pleasant person. I wouldn't have told you if you hadn't asked me. Whether he knew anything or not he has taken his secrets with him, as they say."

" Poor, wretched man. Don't you sometimes think the world's a pretty rotten place, Carolus?"

" No. Never. And you shouldn't, either, after the news you've given me."

Elspeth smiled.

162

" Yes. You're right. But it's when one's happy that things like that seem so rotten."

Carolus finished his whisky and rose to go. It was past midnight and he had eighty miles to drive.

Chapter Sixteen

CAROLUS WOKE TO A BEAUTIFUL SPRING MORNING. THE SUN CAME in his open window and made the events of last night a phantasmagoria.

His first step was to phone Mrs. Stick.

" It's all clear, Mrs. Stick," he told her.

" Are you in the house alone, sir? We'll pop straight down this morning then. I was going to ask you whether my sister and her husband could come with us, just for the week-end?"

Mrs. Stick's sister in Battersea had often been quoted as a model of propriety who, with her undertaker husband, would disapprove of her sister working where there were murders going on, as Mrs. Stick put it. As Carolus was expecting that day to be tackled if not apprehended by the police of Buttsfield for smashing a car window, and questioned none too amicably by those of Brenstead, it did not seem a very apposite time for Mrs. Stick's sister's stay. But he could not refuse.

" Of course, Mrs. Stick," he said. " Have you still got that monster with you?"

" If you mean the young gentleman, sir, it's been a pleasure to have him, and he's met ever such a nice young lady."

Carolus groaned.

" We'll put our things together straight away," said Mrs. Stick, " and be down before lunch."

Carolus now felt himself menaced from four quarters. The Buttsfield police, the Brenstead police, his housekeeper and her formidable sister and almost certainly the headmaster. Of these the most easily placated would be Mr. Gorringer, who would be so consumed with curiosity to know the results of Carolus's researches in Buttsfield that he would forget his disapproval of his senior history master's unfortunate hobby.

In this he was right. Before eleven o'clock that morning Mr. Gorringer appeared at his front door.

" Ah, Deene," he said, " the news of your return has already reached me. I owe it to the keen observation of our school porter, the estimable Muggeridge who noticed your car this morning. How blows the wind?"

" A murder last night," said Carolus. " But come in, headmaster."

Mr. Gorringer stopped dramatically on his way through the door.

" You are not serious, Deene?"

" Yes. Shot through the head from behind, I think."

" These are grim tidings," said Mr. Gorringer. " Who was the victim?"

" A young man named George Catford."

" And the police?"

" I've informed them. They'll probably be over here presently."

Mr. Gorringer seemed to sway a little.

" Here?" he repeated.

"Well, yes. They'll want to know how I found the body."

" You mean that your evidence may be required in court?"

" Just a formality I should think. I happened to be the first to arrive on the scene. Someone has to be."

" Deene, this is a graver matter than you seem to recognise. I was willing to overlook the disgraceful scenes of the other night when I myself was actually threatened with a loaded pistol, but what am I to say to our Board of Governors when one of my staff has to be relieved from his duties to give evidence at an inquest —or even worse at a trial for murder?"

" It might happen to anyone."

" You may be right. The point is that it only happens to you. Could you not have prevented this act of savagery?"

" I might have. I tried, in fact. Have a drink, headmaster?"

" It is far too early in the day for any such indulgence. And yet, in view of the shock . . . perhaps. You have some theory by which to identify the murderer?"

" I know who shot George Catford."

" His murder is connected with the death you were investigating? That of Stick's former employer?"

" Indirectly, yes. But I shall have to give these details to the police when they arrive. I don't want to anticipate that."

Mr. Gorringer, who was facing the window, suddenly paled.

" Deene," he cried. " A police car has just pulled up at the gate and two men in uniform have alighted from it!"

" In uniform? Oh, that's only Buttsfield. Nothing to worry about. I'll let them in."

A grey-haired sergeant entered without removing his peaked cap.

" Your name is Carolus Deene?" he said solemnly. " I have a summons here for you to appear before the Buttsfield magistrates on Friday the twenty-seventh of this month."

" What's the charge?" asked Carolus.

" Wilful damage to property."

" Oh, that car window."

" Yes. That car window. It seems you deliberately smashed it with some heavy implement."

" I had to, yes. I shall of course pay the damage."

" You will doubtless be ordered to do so apart from a fine. We can't have that sort of hooliganism. It is only the fact that we know you to be a person of previous good character . . ."

" I can answer for that, Sergeant," put in Mr. Gorringer.

" That will not be necessary," said the sergeant curtly. " We have made our own enquiries." He turned to Carolus. "You have the summons. That will be all."

The sergeant strode importantly to the door.

"Is there no end to this?" asked Mr. Gorringer, when he had gone. "Wilful damage to property. Hooliganism in a member of my staff! Deene, you are driving me to desperate remedies. Much as I value your services to the school . . . But another car has stopped at your gate. What new embarrassment awaits us?"

Carolus looked out.

"It's only Mrs. Stick's sister from Battersea," he said calmly. "And her husband. An undertaker, I understand."

Mr. Gorringer was moved to heavy humour.

"I cannot but think it an appropriate profession for your housekeeper's relative," he said. "But the person approaching scarcely resembles an undertaker, I should have thought."

Carolus could only agree. Mrs. Stick's brother-in-law was a floridly happy-looking individual in a cloth cap while his wife was a stout blonde in her fifties whose trousers fitted so tightly round an enormous bottom that no one could have called them slacks. They were both smiling cheerfully as Mrs. Stick led them to the front door.

"Worthy people, I daresay," said the headmaster. "I feel, however, that I should be returning to the less eventful atmosphere of the School House. Did I understand you to say that you would be required to give an exposition of your researches to the police, Deene?"

"I should think so. Why? Do you want to hear it?"

"It is not that I wish to do so, but that I feel it my duty. It will not be the first time I have been called upon to protect the good name of the school we both serve."

"If the C.I.D. man in charge is at all reasonable I'll let you know. It's quite an interesting story though rather a gruesome one."

"Then à tout à l'heure, Deene. I shall await your summons."

When the headmaster had gone Mrs. Stick entered, followed by her sister and brother-in-law. Mrs. Stick seemed preoccupied.

167

"I should like to introduce my sister," she said. "And Mr. Grimthorpe."

"We've heard so much about you, Mr. Deene. We've followed all your cases. It must be ever so interesting to investigate crime like that. I tell my sister she's a lucky girl to work where so much is going on."

"Mrs. Stick has always told me you disapprove of it," said Carolus mischievously.

"She doesn't have to put up with it like I do." Mrs. Stick sounded sullen. "Not with never knowing if it's a murderer coming to the door."

"I don't say I should like that," said Mrs. Grimthorpe. "But think of knowing what's happening before the papers get hold of it! My husband says the same. He's always reading about some crime or other."

"Yes. I must say I like a good murder," said Mr. Grimthorpe genially. "Got anything on hand at the moment, Mr. Deene?"

"Now that's enough of that!" said Mrs. Stick. "As if I hadn't enough to put up with, what with Stick pushing himself in. I'm ashamed of you, Edie, really I am."

Mrs. Grimthorpe smiled.

"Oh, don't be so old-fashioned," she said. "You talk like your auntie used to. We like to be with it, Mr. Deene. Good luck to you, I say, if you know more than the police do. Anyway, it's very kind of you to ask us down for a couple of days. We've often wondered how my sister could spend her life in a musty old town like Newminster!"

"I always say, you want to know how the other half live," pronounced Mr. Grimthorpe. "I couldn't do without the Dogs, myself."

Mrs. Stick was making desperate signs to her sister and after some minutes was successful in ushering her cheerful relatives from the room.

"If I'd known how it would Turn Out," she told Carolus when they had gone, "I'd never have asked them down. I don't know what's come over my sister at all. She was always the one who thought what people would say. It was as much as you dared to have a bit of a joke with her when we were girls. It must be since her husband sold his business. One of the big combines have taken it over, it seems, and they think of nothing but enjoying themselves. I'll do what I can for lunch but there's not much time."

"That's all right, Mrs. Stick. Where's Priggley?"

"That's another thing, sir. I don't know what's come over the young gentleman. He's always been so quiet since I've known him, but he seems to have taken to my sister and her husband and now he's as bad as they are. Mr. Grimthorpe says he knows more about the Dogs than what he does and between them they've been winning every night and staying out till all hours. What they find to talk about I *don't* know."

"I do," said Carolus.

"I suppose men are all the same," said Mrs. Stick with some hostility. "Not that he isn't always respectful to me, only you should see the way the three of them carry on."

A sound of loud laughter came from the Sticks' sitting-room.

"Hark at them!" said Mrs. Stick disapprovingly. "Like a lot of magpies. It's a good thing we're not all like that."

It was not until six o'clock that day that Carolus received the call he was expecting from the C.I.D. He had been wondering what their attitude would be. They might quite seriously suspect him. They knew from Beckett that he had discovered the body. They would have found out by now that he had been staying in the same house as George Catford and they could easily have discovered that he had a firearms certificate for a pistol. Even if they did not suspect him their attitude might be hostile, even threatening. They could take him in for enquiries and expect to learn everything he knew by a gruelling cross-examination. But if they were intelligent, or knew that on previous occasions he had been helpful to the police without wishing to claim any credit for what he had done, they might treat him with consideration and friendliness and learn much more than they would by any other method.

When they arrived, two large, serious, middle-aged men, Carolus quickly perceived what tactics they had decided to adopt.

It was one used frequently with suspects, particularly young and inexperienced ones, and with them was usually successful. It was known among criminals as ' The good bloke and the bastard '. One appeared reasonable, friendly, kind, the other acted as though he could with difficulty be withheld by his associate from carrying out all sorts of threats from beating-up to arrest. This combination often broke down the resistance of juvenile delinquents. Carolus realised that he was going to find it difficult to avoid discomfort and perhaps humiliation. However, at the moment he held all the high cards for since the result of the inquest on Parador the police had dropped the case while he had worked on it. Moreover he knew the truth, and though they already probably had inklings of it he could save them a great deal of time.

They were of equal rank. One showed Carolus his official identity card, Detective-Inspector Hemingway, and introduced the other, Detective-Inspector Haggard. Hemingway was to be the good bloke, evidently.

" You made a report to the sergeant in charge at Brenstead last night, I believe, Mr. Deene?"

" That's right."

" You had discovered the body of a dead man in the car park of the Great Ring?"

" Yes."

" What were you doing there?" asked Haggard fiercely.

Carolus answered neither flippantly nor evasively, but took the wind out of the detective's sails by saying calmly, " I had followed Catford there."

" You followed him there! What for?"

" I wanted to see whom he would meet."

" What business was that of yours?" shouted Haggard.

" Just a minute, Mr. Deene," put in Hemingway in a concilia-tory tone, as though it was Carolus who had shown excitement. " Are we to understand you knew the dead man?"

" Oh yes. I knew him. I had moved into his boarding-house especially to make his acquaintance."

" Why?" asked Haggard.

" That is a question I'm not at the moment prepared to answer."

" Oh, you're not. Do you realise that you're under very grave suspicion in this case?"

" No. I do not. I have more respect for the intelligence of the police than that."

" Then why are you refusing to give us information?"

Hemingway smiled.

" You see, Mr. Deene, we have a heavy responsibility. We naturally want to know what you can tell us. Catford was shot through the head with a pistol at close range."

" Yes. I thought so from the casual look I took at the corpse. Probably while he was putting his motor-cycle on the stand, wasn't it?"

" Well ask the questions," said Haggard. " Have you got a revolver?"

" Yes. Want to see it?"

Carolus crossed to his desk and was about to open a drawer when Haggard said, " Never mind that now."

" Now look here," said Carolus. " You're going about this altogether the wrong way. You know perfectly well I didn't shoot Catford. You also believe, quite rightly, that I've got a lot of information for you . . ."

" So we're going about it the wrong way?" said Haggard sarcastically. " What way would you suggest we went about it?"

" I'll tell you. It's quite simple. First we all have a drink. Then we relax and start again. Then instead of one of you wheedling and the other bullying you let me tell you the story in my own way. Then if you have any questions I can answer I will undertake to answer them. Because, you know, really we shan't get anywhere like this."

The two men exchanged glances.

" What story?" asked Haggard, still with hostility. " We haven't come here to listen to fairy stories, you know. We've come to get the truth."

" It's quite a long story," said Carolus. " But it's not about The Good People. On the contrary I don't think I've met a more

171

horribly cold-blooded murder in the whole of my experience."

" You talk of your experience. If you'd had what we've had you wouldn't think so much of the murder of George Catford. We've both known worse than that."

" Catford? I wasn't thinking of that. An everyday little affair. I was thinking of the murder of Felix Parador. But let's have that drink we were talking about."

He went to the house phone and asked Mrs. Stick for the tray of drinks she usually brought in at this time. It was just as she was entering that Haggard said sarcastically, " So Felix Parador was murdered, was he?"

" Yes," said Carolus. " Oh, Mrs. Stick, telephone Mr. Gorringer, will you, and tell him the two detective-inspectors I was expecting are here if he likes to come across."

Mrs. Stick gave Carolus a withering look.

" Well," she said, but she infused the monosyllable with seething indignation.

" What will you have, Detective-Inspector? And you? Yes, Parador was murdered. Soda or water? So was Catford, of course, but that was a simpler matter. Your good health."

" I give it up," said Haggard. " I've never heard anything like this in my life. I don't know what I'm doing letting you rattle on. I must be out of my mind. When I ask questions I expect to get them answered, not listen to a lot of fantasy."

" You'll get them answered," said Carolus.

" I hear you're in trouble with the Buttsfield police as well," went on Haggard. " Smashing windows or something. Do you go about smashing windows, Mr. Deene?"

" Not really. But look at that one," and he pointed to the window through which he had fired.

" This was done by a revolver shot!" said Haggard, examining it.

" Yes. Fired from where you are now. It didn't hit anyone, though."

Haggard turned to Hemingway. " We oughtn't to be listening to this man," he said. " He's barking mad."

" Better hear him out."

172

At that moment Mr. Gorringer entered, beaming.

"Good evening, gentlemen," he said. "We are in for a rare treat, I opine. Our good Deene is about to take us into his confidence with one of his famous elucidations. Splendid. As an old hand, let me warn you that there will be moments which will seem to you frankly incredible. There will be suggestions which you will think conflict with reason. But be patient and you will find that all becomes admirably clear."

If Detective-Inspector Hemingway had looked with wonder at Detective-Inspector Haggard before, they now stared at one another and at Mr. Gorringer with amazement.

"I came here to ask some perfectly simple questions about the circumstances of a man's death last night," said Haggard.

Mr. Gorringer raised his hand.

"You will be given a perfectly simple explanation," he said graciously. "Come, my dear Deene, proceed!"

Chapter Seventeen

" WHAT FIRST INTERESTED ME ABOUT THIS CASE," BEGAN CAROLUS quietly, " was the man in the railway compartment. Here we have Parador's five fellow commuters waiting for him to travel to London with them when instead comes a mysterious creature in dark glasses dressed all in black who announced that Parador won't be coming.

" It has been pointed out that he might have been a stranger justifying himself for taking an empty seat and meant merely that *no* one would be coming so near the departure of the train, but the men who heard him did not get this impression at all. They felt, even at the time, that he *knew* something. When I began to learn about his movements from the car park man at the station I became convinced that he had deliberately chosen that carriage for some purpose of his own. (By the way, car parks play a very large part in this case as you will see, just as they play a large, far too large, part in our lives.)

" He rode up that morning, left his Criterion motor-cycle, registration number BYY 018, and bought a first-class ticket and entered this carriage. Moreover, as I discovered later, he had been out on his motor-cycle the night before and had only been back to his aunt's private hotel to put on the black suit, socks and tie she had bought him for his uncle's funeral a year ago. Finally, I knew from the car park man that he had only had a couple of hours or so in London because he was back on a train which left London at one o'clock, and after trying to ask some questions about commuters which the car park man would not answer, he set off on his motor-cycle.

" I was convinced then that when he said in that deep voice of his ' He won't be coming ' and, being asked what he meant, repeated, ' Just that. He won't be coming ', he was not excusing himself for taking an unofficially reserved seat, but speaking deliberately to one or more of the five men present. And that he had taken great trouble and gone to some expense to make that announcement in that particularly impressive and dramatic way.

" Why? What could his object be? There could really be only one—intimidation. And intimidation, it was fairly safe, though not *quite* safe to say, with the object of blackmail. He knew something about one or more of those five men in connection with the death of Felix Parador which put him in a position of power. He was showing his future victim or victims that he knew it and was going to act on it. That much was fairly obvious and nothing else accounts for the extraordinary behaviour of George Catford that morning.

" But what did he know? And which of the five men was concerned? And how concerned—directly or indirectly? This I decided to discover, and I set out in my own way, listening to a good deal of idle chatter and irrelevant information in order to do so."

" A moment!" said Mr. Gorringer. " How did you identify this man?"

Carolus smiled.

" The police were good enough to do that for me. I had the number of the motor-cycle he had left in the station car park that morning and I faked a small accident to my car, reporting his as the other party. They discovered the owner and his address.

175

I shall really have to apologise to Sergeant Beckett but there was no other way of learning the facts quickly."

The faces of Hemingway and Haggard remained unmoved.

"From this point, and for a long time, I was reduced to guess-work. I was faced with a number of questions, some of which were unanswerable, and yet I believed that some theory existed which would make sense of *all* of them. If Catford knew something important enough to enable him to attempt such a bare-faced piece of blackmail it could only be one thing—the fact that Parador had not died by his own hand. Yet how else? Who could possibly be responsible? For what motive? I tried all manner of combinations, but nothing seemed to fit. Until, on a certain occasion I will describe to you, I heard one sentence of nine words which satisfied me that one of the possibilities I had seen was not a possibility at all but a certainty. Thereafter everything fitted into the pattern and I knew the truth.

"I must start with a love-story. Two years ago James Rumble lost his wife and, a lonely and introspective man, he fell desperately in love with Elspeth Parador. I have seen them together and apart and I have no hesitation in saying that this was more than sincere love, it was blind, agonising, ruthless, the love of Abelard and Heloise, if you like, or if you are more cynical, of Thompson and Bywaters. For a long time it was secret, but secrecy only added to its intensity. The two had to see one another occasionally and their method of covering up on this was for Elspeth to appear to be equally friendly with several men in the place, entertain them and talk about them to Felix, the principle of safety in numbers. Boggett told me of these, Hopelady, Thriver, the younger Limpole. Even to Boggett's crafty and observant eye, James Rumble was only one of the men who occasionally came to the Old Manor. For over a year Elspeth and Rumble—I can only use the common but pregnant expression—were madly in love."

"What proof have you of this?" asked Haggard impatiently.

"Only my own observation and instincts—and the events which followed."

"But let us cry halt for a moment," said Mr. Gorringer to

smooth over this awkward moment. "It is the custom of those privileged to hear Deene's lucid expositions to give him a moment's respite *de temps en temps* while we refresh ourselves."

"I've heard no lucid explanations yet," grumbled Haggard. "Only an admission of having brought a false charge against a motor-cyclist and a lot about love based on personal instinct. What I want to know . . ."

"What you want to know, you *will* know; rest assured of that, my dear sir, and in the meantime let me fill your glass."

Carolus, looking rather seedy and troubled, said nothing while the headmaster was busy. Then he went on.

"Elspeth was so taken up with James Rumble and the difficulties of keeping the secret of their love in a place hungry for gossip, that she did not even know her husband was keeping Henrietta Ballard and going to Buttsfield to see her. Yet she had been fond of Felix and perhaps in her way was fond of him still. Love like that, obsessive and aching, can blind people to everything else. She was actress enough to follow her usual life so far as others could see, even so far as Felix could see.

"But this could not continue. As time passed she and James Rumble imagined for themselves a sort of paradise, somewhere abroad, perhaps in Spain, where they could be together for the rest of their lives. At first, perhaps, they thought of it as 'one day', meaning after Felix's death, for Felix was a considerably older man and believed at one time that he had cancer. At first it was as harmless as that—the Great Possibility in the future. But months passed and Dr. Sporlott decided that there was no sign of cancer and at last, in desperation, they began testing each other by allusions and suggestions. 'One day' became 'if anything were to happen to Felix'. Finally they decided to kill him."

"Good gracious me!" said Mr. Gorringer.

"Once they had admitted to one another that this was their intention, they began to plan how it could be done without the slightest risk to themselves. They were not going to have their paradise snatched away by years of imprisonment for murder. And they nearly succeeded. So nearly that even now one of them, at least, may escape the consequences.

" The plan was to give Felix an overdose of sleeping pills disguised as something else, then make it appear that he had committed suicide. They took their time. First they had to obtain a powerful antibiotic, and decided on Opilactic. Elspeth suggested a holiday in Tangier where, she must have known, chemists sell this and other drugs without insisting on a doctor's prescription. She may have obtained the information from Scotter; if so, it was with great subtlety and she certainly would not have got the tablets from him. What she may have bought, some considerable time ago—and this the police will doubtless ascertain if they think it necessary—is something sold in those little capsules made of rice-paper in which a sufficient dose of Opilactic, pounded in a mortar, could be inserted. This is, of course, only a guess, but Felix was a man who took medicines easily.

" There were other preparations to make. Rumble was aware that Bert Holey who kept the local filling-station was in the habit of noticing the mileage and petrol level of his clients' cars, and not wishing this observation to be made of his, picked a quarrel with Holey and filled his car elsewhere. They also saw less of one another, so that Elspeth in introducing Rumble to me was able to say that they ' scarcely knew each other ' before Felix's death without fear that she would be contradicted, and Rumble could say ' it's only since this happened I've been seeing much of Elspeth '.

" I think they fixed the time by a certain eventuality. Felix occasionally drove over to see Dr. Kumar Shant in Buttsfield, and the doctor would give him a prescription which Elspeth would take to Scotter next day. Felix would then be expecting to take medicine when he came down in the evening and Elspeth could give him the capsule or capsules full of Opilactic without arousing his suspicion. It was unlikely that this *would* be aroused since he trusted Elspeth, but they had to think of every possible eventuality. The only risk she ran now was that Felix might grumble at the size of the capsule and decide to ring up Dr. Kumar Shant before taking it. But it was a small risk. As I knew from Magnus Parador, one of Felix's little meannesses was over the telephone. He hated making unnecessary calls and would swallow the capsules without question.

"Yes. They nearly brought it off. And as usual it was chance that defeated them. For how were they to know that on the day they had chosen, the very day on which Elspeth had taken Kumar Shant's prescription to Scotter, Felix Parador would call at his lawyer's to sign a new will? And how were they to know of George Catford and his habit of motor-cycling to lonely places to indulge in megalomaniac dreams?"

Mrs. Stick, who must have been waiting at the door for a pause in Carolus's narrative, entered.

"What about dinner?" she asked firmly. "*They've* all gone to the pictures and I've got yours ready."

She gave a hostile look at the rest of the assembly.

"There are four of us, Mrs. Stick."

"Yes, I know there are but there's not enough, I'm afraid." This was so unlike Mrs. Stick that it could only be explained by her hostility to the police.

Hemingway and Haggard both made protestations. Carolus was not to bother about them.

"What about some sandwiches, Mrs. Stick? We can eat them while we are talking."

Knowing that her disapproval of policemen as visitors was only slightly less than her horror of 'murderers', Carolus feared this might bring another outbreak from Mrs. Stick. But her pride as a caterer was too strong for her.

"I might manage a few sandwiches," she admitted, "but you'll have to wait some time because there's nothing ready and Stick's gone to the pictures with the rest of them. I don't know what's come over him. I really don't. He usually won't leave the telly. Well, I'll see what I can do."

She left them and Mr. Gorringer shook his head.

"You are fortunate indeed, my dear Deene. The help we are able to get at the School House is meagre. Meagre in the extreme."

Haggard coughed and looked at his watch, but Hemingway said, "It's very kind of you to be so hospitable, Mr. Deene. But you will understand we have to get back to Brenstead. I'm not denying that what you are telling us may turn out to be useful, but . . ."

"Detective-Inspector, relax!" commanded Mr. Gorringer.

"That's all very well," said Haggard. "But we happen to be on duty."

"Ah! Magic word! But I assure you Deene will reach the end of his peroration in his own good time."

Carolus, as though he had not heard this altercation, continued quietly.

"Yes, Felix Parador went to Thriver's office in the City that afternoon to sign a new will. Only three people were aware of it, Parador himself, Thriver, and Thriver's confidential clerk, all men accustomed to keeping secrets. There was good reason for secrecy in this case for Parador had arranged to leave a thousand pounds a year for life to his mistress, Henrietta Ballard. He was also cutting out two minor beneficiaries for reasons which seemed to him adequate, Dr. Sporlott for what he considered a breach of confidence, and Hopelady for a practical joke which had shown him at a disadvantage. These are not things which would make many men change their wills, but Parador was in some ways unusual and had had an unusual life. According to his own sense of justice (or was it humour?) he was fair to his godson who would lose nothing, in fact probably gain by the change.

"Thriver told me that he was quite himself, quite cheerful that afternoon and a boy in his own office remembered and told the Coroner of how he had fooled about with a hat too small for him. He came down in the train, gave Bill Flood the same impression as he gave Thriver, then set off in his car. From that time to the next morning at ten when a policeman found his dead body in his own car in the parking place of the Great Ring, nothing positive is known of his movements.

"But there was one fact which I found very helpful. His car, when it was driven back to Brenstead after his death, registered, according to Bert Holey, only twenty miles more on the speedometer. This was the distance to the Great Ring and back.

Wherever he was between the arrival of his train at Brenstead and the arrival of his car at the Great Ring, he was not driving about the countryside.

"But we know where he was. From the station he drove, as he did every evening, to his home. Among the plans made by Elspeth and Rumble was one—I think ill-advised from their point of view—that Elspeth should say she had received a call from Felix to say he was not coming down that night. The idea was to account for her not being anxious when he—according to the account she would give—did not appear. But there is nothing but Elspeth's word for this call and no reason to think it was ever made. Felix arrived home, was welcomed by Elspeth and, according to his custom as told me by Magnus, probably had a couple of stiff whiskies which would make deadlier and quicker the effect of the Opilactic.

"Everything, on the surface, was as usual. Then probably Elspeth said, 'By the way I got your pills from Scotter today. You have to take two this evening'. Felix may have said, 'What pills?', and she, 'The ones Dr. Kumar Shant ordered for you'. And Felix swallowed the capsule, or two capsules if that was necessary. I don't know how long after that he died but I have no doubt experts could tell to within half an hour. I don't think it's very important, anyway."

Haggard could scarcely restrain himself.

"But what proof have you of all this?"

Carolus smiled rather sadly.

"I'm afraid I'm telling it rather as I see it. Novelist fashion. But I *do* know that he went to his home and that only later was he taken out to the Great Ring. I think I shall be able to convince you of that in a moment, if you'll let me go on in my own way."

"I'm bound to confess," boomed Mr. Gorringer, "that you seem to be taking a great deal on yourself, Deene, by so positively accusing a woman of high repute. Did you yourself find her so base?"

"I found her charming. But then she had been an actress. Ah, here is Mrs. Stick with our sandwiches."

"Just a minute, sir; there's another tray to come. These are the smoked salmon and there's some caviar there by the headmaster. I've left the foy grass whole on the ice so you can help yourselves. I didn't know what you'd like to drink so I've had this couple of bottles of Rosy on the ice for you."

"Kingly providence!" said Mr. Gorringer. "Mrs. Stick, you excel yourself."

"I did what I could in the time," said Mrs. Stick modestly. "I thought if you must talk about murders and that you might as well have something to do it on."

"You are not interested?" asked Mr. Gorringer with his mouth full.

"I don't want to hear of such things," said Mrs. Stick. "I've had quite enough of it as it is. You'll ring if you want anything else, sir?"

Carolus nodded and ate and drank in a preoccupied way. Then almost before they had finished eating, he went on.

"Elspeth Parador was an astonishing woman as I had reason to know later. She coolly waited until her husband was dead then telephoned to Rumble to come at once, according to plan. At a certain time that night, which you gentlemen will be able to establish for yourselves, the two of them took the body of Felix out to the yard at the back. They may have prepared a stretcher for this—I don't know. They put him in the seat next to the driver's in his own car which one of them drove, while the other followed in Rumble's. I rather think, because it fits in with my conception of her character, that it was Elspeth who drove the dead man.

"This was not so risky as it seems, for if they were stopped they had a perfectly good story ready. Felix had gone to his study and swallowed a whole bottle of Opilactic. They had discovered him and were driving him post haste to his own doctor at Buttsfield. They might have been blamed for not immediately sending for Sporlott who was nearer, but nothing more might have been proved against them. In fact—it's easy to talk after the event—I wonder why they didn't handle it this way in any case, and arrive on Kumar Shant's doorstep with their load. They

182

wouldn't have escaped all suspicion but they might have escaped conviction.

" But they had made other plans. They found the car park of the Great Ring empty as they were confident it would be. They pushed the corpse of Felix into the driving seat, left an empty flask of whisky with him and an empty bottle which had held Opilactic tablets, with one dropped on the floor for the sake of naturalness and got into Rumble's car to return.

" Their story, if they were seen or stopped on the way back, was equally good. Once clear of the Great Ring they could say that Rumble had seen Felix on the train that night and as he had not come home, they had been to Buttsfield to look for his car. Not very convincing but impossible to disprove. But they were not stopped and as far as they knew they were not seen.

" Whether George Catford was actually at the Great Ring with his motor-cycle out of sight, or whether he was on the road and saw *two* cars turn up towards the Great Ring and only *one* emerge from the turning so that he went up to investigate, we shall probably never know. But he knew what they had left there and followed them back to Brenstead. He even went up Manor Lane and saw Rumble drop Elspeth at her home, then followed him back to his own, noting the address. He was not quite as accurate as he thought about this because some nights later, when he came either to reconnoitre or to see Rumble, he got the wrong house and was seen by Patsy Thriver peering in the window of their house, which is next door to Rumble's.

" The rest of his movements we know. He returned to Buttsfield, changed into his alarming black clothes and put on his dark glasses, then rode back to Brenstead in the early morning to watch outside Rumble's house. This, he believed, was the Great Chance for which, he told me, he had always held himself in readiness."

Chapter Eighteen

" To me, the most fascinating thing about investigating a clever crime is to find where the criminal has made his mistake. Fortunately for the course of justice he always makes at least one, and Elspeth Parador and James Rumble soon discovered theirs. They had forgotten to leave Felix's brief-case beside him in the car and it lay where he had left it in the hall of the Old Manor.

" That he had it with him that day we know from two sources —Thriver saw him put the will he had signed in it at his office and Flood held it for him when he opened the door of his car at Brenstead station.

" When did Elspeth discover it? That same night? Or in the morning? It is just possible that the discovery was made by Mrs. Byles or Mrs. Pocock, the two women who come in daily to help at the Old Manor; if so it will be a valuable piece of evidence. Whenever it was, Elspeth must certainly have decided to destroy every trace of it. It would be supposed that someone had stolen it from the car, she hoped, if the question arose at all. Before destroying it she went through the contents and found the new will.

"It is the unexpected which upsets the most careful plans and she and Rumble had made no provision for this. Destroy it? But Henrietta Ballard might know that Felix was leaving her money and would raise heaven and earth to trace the will, which might lead to all sorts of awkward questions. Ironically she had no personal interest in it one way or the other, but she knew Henrietta to be as ruthless as herself. Send it anonymously to Thriver who, she saw, had drawn it up? He would suppose that some repentant thief had returned it, perhaps. In the end, after a fruitless discussion with Rumble, who had his own worries at this time, she decided to keep it hidden and watch the course of events. The inquest must have relieved her mind a little. Suicide was officially accepted as the explanation of Felix's death and she could breathe again.

"Rumble, meanwhile, had been approached by Catford for a very large sum of money. Whether Catford followed him to his office when he left the train that morning, or made his approach by telephone, I cannot guess. But at any rate Rumble stalled. Had he known as much as I came to know of Catford he might have paid up. Catford wanted one big sum to take him somewhere, where he could use that as capital on which to accumulate a fortune. By the time he had failed in this, Rumble and Elspeth would have left the district and after a year, say, his information about what happened that night would not have been much good. I doubt if the police would have re-opened enquiries on a tale told by a man who had been in prison for fraud, and, if they did so, the evidence to support his story would have vanished.

"For a time the two of them were cautious about seeing one another, Elspeth going to Rumble's house at night. I shouldn't be surprised if it was on one of these visits that Elspeth knocked over old Gobler, but I haven't the smallest evidence for that, just noting that it was someone who did not want to stop.

"It was at this point that my housekeeper's husband who had once worked for Parador came to me, and on his persuasion I went to see Magnus Parador and took an interest in the case. I must have been singularly unwelcome to Elspeth and Rumble who, however, were clever enough to appear pleased at my arrival. Elspeth hoped I would get at the truth about Felix and I set to work.

"I had almost nothing to go on. I believed that the man in the train knew something about one of the other passengers but it was little more than a hunch. I put some faith in a brief-case I carried which was an exact duplicate of Felix's, but I knew it might fail to get reactions. I believed Felix Parador had been murdered and I suspected his wife for no better reason than that I did not see where he could have gone when he left the train that evening except home. I had to regard his five fellow travellers with almost equal suspicion and it happened that they provided a fine collection of red herrings, for all five of them, Thriver, Dogman, the brothers Limpole, and Rumble were out that night—Dogman, Thriver and Rumble being seen at The Royal Oak and the brothers Limpole chasing about the country-side looking for their sister. For a time I had at least to recognise that Sporlott and Hopelady had some sort of motive, but frankly I did not take them very very seriously as suspects. In fact for a time I was floundering."

"We appreciate your modesty, Deene. But let us . . ."

"Yes," said Carolus. "Let us. I'm dry. I didn't realise that I should keep you so long, gentlemen."

"That's all right, Mr. Deene," said Hemingway, and even Haggard said, "We'd certainly like to hear you out now we've gone so far."

Carolus lit a cheroot.

"There were several things that pointed my way, but nothing absolutely reliable. The brief-case was not in the car when it was found and if it was a thief who had taken it surely he would have also taken the money, about £70, in Parador's pocket-case? There was an empty whisky flask, the idea being that Parador had swallowed the contents in taking his pills. This could have been intended to account for the whisky which the post-mortem would reveal, the whisky which Felix had actually drunk on arrival at the Old Manor. Thriver remembered the flask being emptied at his office. But there were ways of accounting for this other than the way I saw it.

186

" Then there was the little I discovered about the movements of Elspeth and Rumble that evening. Thriver heard the sound of television and radio as he approached the house and Elspeth did not ask him in as she usually did, but told him she was going to bed. This fitted with the probable timing—Felix was dead or dying and Rumble was with her. But it *proved* nothing. Thriver surprised Elspeth by saying he was going to The Royal Oak and soon after he arrived there Rumble came in for a drink. Again it was possible that he looked in as some sort of alibi before going with Elspeth to take the body to the Great Ring, but there was no certainty about this.

" More relevant, and hard to account for in any way but the truth was Boggett's story of the cars he heard late that night. *Two* going out of Manor Lane, which would be Elspeth taking the body of Felix and Rumble following her to bring her back, *one* returning followed by a motor-cycle, which would be Rumble and Elspeth returning followed by Catford, and *one* coming out of the lane again followed by a motor-cycle—Rumble going home with Catford following to see where he lived. All very nice but lacking the final touch of definite application. There was even the fact that Rumble, who rarely ate much in the evening, that evening finished off all that was left for him, which suggested to me that he had burnt or otherwise destroyed it to avoid leaving his meal untouched. But what was that worth as evidence?

" I noticed, too, how conveniently invisible from anywhere, certainly from any window, was the yard at the back of the Old Manor where the cars of both Felix and Rumble must have stood that evening. It was an ideal place to keep them during the hours when no one must know that either of the men was in the house and the body could have been put in the car there. Even Rumble's hysteria with me, when he found I had been questioning Elspeth, *could* be explained by his love and consideration for her which, I for one, never doubted. I had my theory but as Detective-Inspector Haggard is about to tell me, there was no proof worth a cold carrot.

" For a time it continued like that. Elspeth and Rumble

decided that it would be best to let it be seen that they were in love. They thought, probably rightly, that more suspicion would be aroused by clandestine meetings, if they were discovered, than an open, even proud, admission. They also decided to return the will anonymously to Thriver. They were not much worried about me, but Henrietta Ballard was a different matter.

"Very indicative was Elspeth's reaction to the brief-case. When she saw it in my hand at her house she never batted an eyelid. If she had known nothing of what had happened to Felix's she would have remarked on it. Couldn't have helped doing so. It could only be that old-fashioned thing a guilty conscience which made her affect to ignore it. But this again was not proof.

"Then, in a place and at a time when I least expected it, came what I needed. At Chatty Dogman's party there appeared dramatically the woman Felix Parador had been keeping. She had heard from Thriver that according to the only will in his possession she had been left nothing and, drunk or drugged or both, she had come to raise hell with Elspeth as publicly as possible. Elspeth kept her head while she raged but when she had gone, as any woman might, she broke down. Her remarkable self-possession left her and she let fall those words which, if the death penalty had not been abolished, would have hanged her as surely as Edith Thompson's love-letters hanged her. Henrietta had shouted, 'he left me without a sou', and Elspeth, in the hysteria of reaction after she had gone, said, 'and he *didn't* leave her without a sou'.

"Remember, this was before the will had been sent back to Thriver. It proved that Elspeth had seen the will. It proved that Felix had been to his house that night. It proved—to my mind at least—that Elspeth and her lover had murdered him."

There was silence for a moment, then Haggard said quietly, "There *are* other possible explanations, you know."

"There are. But so remote that they needn't be seriously considered. What I wanted was enough to persuade the police to re-open the case. Once they did so they would find the evidence which in their position of authority, and with their expertise they *can* find, while I cannot. Which you *will* find, I believe, when you have heard the rest."

There was a long pause which even Mr. Gorringer did not interrupt.

" I was not yet satisfied and there was still George Catford. I deliberately told Elspeth that I had unearthed Catford and was going to see him. This put her and Rumble in a desperate position. If I was once able to make Catford talk they were both lost. They decided to risk everything on an attempt to kill me that night. I had told Elspeth that my housekeeper would be away and they hoped to find me alone in the house. There were risks here—that someone might note the number of their car or that they might be seen. They guarded against these as best they could. Rumble had his old overalls from the time he rode a motor-cycle (as I had heard from Thriver), and Elspeth, I would like to bet, still had the things she needed to put on an effective make-up. But whatever the risks, they had to take them. The alternative was failure and imprisonment—the sure, the only alternative. So they arrived here that evening and found the curtains of this room undrawn and the room lit only by fire-light.

" I don't know how much Rumble saw when he looked in but not enough to distinguish me and shoot me from there. He tried to enter by the front door but found himself blocked by a stranger. Quite desperate now, he levelled his revolver at the headmaster's chest and forced him to retreat. But when I shot at the sky through that window he lost his nerve. Heaven knows what he thought, if he thought at all, but his first anxiety was for Elspeth waiting in the car outside. Perhaps he thought I had shot at her, though I could not even see the car from here. He dashed out and they drove away.

" As you know, I emptied the house after that. I expected that as soon as Rumble and Elspeth saw that no newspaper carried any account of the incident they would conclude, as was indeed the case, that if anyone heard the sound of a shot they had put it down to a car backfiring. They could now only hope that Catford would be greedy enough to keep the thing to himself in order to

189

obtain the money they promised him, and telephoned him that very evening to tell him the money was being arranged and would be handed over in a day or two. Whether one or both of them came here again on the following night I don't know. In their state of mind at that time they were capable of it."

" You were taking serious risks, Deene," said Mr. Gorringer reproachfully. " Of both your own life and . . . others."

Carolus went on rather hurriedly.

" I was lucky enough to obtain a room in the boarding-house owned by Catford's aunt in which he lived. I learned a great deal about that young man—excellent material for neo-nazi recruitment. My miscalculation was in respect of Rumble. I thought he would have the sense to hand over the money, however much it was. That was the only way in which I could account for those few days' delay. If he had done so it would have meant that I could go at last to the police with a case of murder and one of blackmail neatly tied up. But Rumble and Elspeth had decided otherwise. They did not believe themselves suspected of anything, for I had maintained the friendliest relations with Elspeth. In that case there would be nothing in the world to connect either of them with the murder of Catford, and their dream of life together would come true.

" It was decided that Rumble should do this alone. He telephoned to the number Catford had given him, his aunt's, and told Catford he was ready to hand over. Catford himself was wary enough to take no chances of hidden tape-recorders or witnesses and arranged the meeting at the Great Ring. He set off on his motor-cycle and I followed, but was unfortunately delayed by a car parked in front of mine. I smashed its window and got away as fast as possible but was too late. I arrived to see the vicar's car, which Rumble had stolen for the purpose, coming out of the lane from the Great Ring. I found that Catford had been shot through the back of the head while he had been lifting his motor-cycle on its stand.

" Back in Brenstead I stopped only to confirm that it was the vicar's car that had been used and learn from his wife that Hopelady had been in bed with flu since yesterday afternoon.

That could, of course, be checked with the doctor . . ."

"It has been," said Hemingway quietly.

"I then went to report the finding of Catford's body to the police. My report was received with a certain scepticism, perhaps because the registration number of the motor-cycle was the one I had given when I was trying to trace Catford."

"You could scarcely expect anything else, Mr. Deene."

"I didn't. But I had to make my report credible enough for a police car to go out at once."

"Which it did, of course. You will probably be surprised to know that James Rumble has already been charged with the murder of George Catford."

Mr. Gorringer could not keep silence.

"*I* am surprised, at all events! This will be the first time I have known one of Deene's theories actually anticipated!"

"It has nothing to do with Mr. Deene's theories. Police work is less complicated than that, and more practical, perhaps. We do not look for these elaborate theories based on instincts, intuitions and so on, but we do have our simple methods of procedure. James Rumble was seen returning the vicar's car to its place by a very observant witness, Miss Nora Limpole, which set in motion other enquiries, finger-print tests and so on. Rumble has already made a statement. His chief object seems to be to take all the blame on himself. Not," added Haggard patronisingly, "that yours has not been a very interesting story, Mr. Deene."

"He can't take all the blame himself," said Carolus. "I was about to tell you that after I had reported to the police I went to the Old Manor. Rumble's coat was hanging in the hall, but Elspeth said he was 'staying in for an early night'. Clearly he had come to report and was somewhere in the house. I felt his presence and knew that if I gave any indication that I knew the truth I should have had it. On the contrary, I said that I had abandoned the case and Catford had taken his secrets to the grave. I've never in my life felt nearer to an unpleasant death."

"I hope you never *are* nearer, my dear Deene. But I'm bound to point out that such risks come of meddling in affairs which

191

the police are perfectly capable of handling without your intervention."

"Not at all. They knew that Rumble killed Catford, that's all. They did not know why. They did not know that he and Elspeth also killed Felix Parador."

"We don't know that now, Mr. Deene. You have provided us with some very interesting possibilities. That is all. There is no proof."

"Oh, *proof*," said Carolus, almost contemptuously. "I leave that to you. You have all the facilities. Proof is a technical matter."

"Which follows in the wake of inspiration; is that it, Mr. Deene?" said Hemingway, smiling grimly. "You may be right. But it would never do for us to start thinking like that. What you have done here is to suggest a possible motive for the murder of Catford. It is not unlikely that we should have had that within twenty-four hours. We haven't yet gone through Catford's papers."

The two detective-inspectors rose to leave. Carolus sank back exhausted in his chair.

"You think they will act on your excellent suggestions?" queried Mr. Gorringer.

"It's not a matter of that. The whole thing follows automatically now. Elspeth and Rumble will both get life sentences of course."

"For murder," Mr. Gorringer reminded him.

"For a very cruel and pitiless murder and for a savage and ruthless one."

"Then what is troubling you?"

"Not any injustice. The sentence will be most just. But something else. You know, when I met them, they both seemed such thoroughly *nice* people."

"I catch your drift," said Mr. Gorringer nodding solemnly. "You mean that what we call nice people may not be nice at all. May, in fact, be . . ."

"Murderers," said Carolus wearily and emptied his glass at a gulp.

CPSIA information can be obtained
at www.ICGtesting.com
Printed in the USA
LVOW11s0446210317
527928LV00002B/17/P